BLACK SCARFACE IV

This work is a work of fiction. Any resemblance to real people, living or dead, actual events, establishments, or locales are intended to give the fiction a sense of reality and authenticity. Other names, characters, places and incidents are either products of the author's imagination or are used fictitiously. Those fictionalized events and incidents that involve real persons did not occur and/or may be set in the future.

Published by DASAINT ENTERTAINMENT
Po Box 97 Bala Cynwyd, PA 19004
Website: www.dasaintentertainment.com

My Dedication:

This book is dedicated to all the prisoners locked away in State and Federal facilities. There was a time in my life when I was a prisoner just like you. For ten lonely years I was trapped in a cell, hundreds, even thousands of miles away from my city, my family, and my children and friends.

My crimes had finally caught up to me and just like so many others before me, and many after me, I had to face the wrath of the U.S. Government. It was my time to pay my debt and to suffer the consequences for my actions.

I was a young hustler from West Philly that lived and would die by the code of the streets. It was that same code that had become my demise.

I've witnessed death snatch away so many of my friends, while prison grabbed up the rest. If I knew all that I know now, or had a father to guide and teach me the ways of the world; maybe life would be different. Yet I've realized that I chose this life. I had to learn some hard lessons but God has been with me on every pathway I've taken.

I have learned that I'm a survivor and a solider in God's army. I've learned never to give up in the face of adversity and to always fight for my beliefs. I've learned that even in darkness light shines on all those who believe…and I am a believer.

-Jimmy DaSaint

**"Finally my brethren, be strong in the Lord
and in the power of his might.
Put on the whole armor of God,
that ye may be able to stand against
the wiles of the devil."**

-Ephesians 6:10-11

Chapter 1
2:17 A.M.
Christmas Day
Hahnemann University Hospital

With lightening force the 9mm bullet exploded from the gun and sped swiftly into Face's chest. The impact was so powerful that it knocked him so far back into his chair, as if he was being held down by captures. He began to gasp for air as his airways felt if they were closing shut. Face clutched his chest; feeling the heat and pain rise up through his body. His mind began to slow down as he realized someone had just shot him.

Just a few footsteps away, Arianna, who was still aiming her gun at Face, stood frozen in time. She was silent and filled with shock. She hadn't expected the gun to fire as quietly as it had. It was very smooth and the popping sound was brief and could have been misconstrued as a hard object falling onto the ground. But she was not afraid. Fear made no introductions into her soul as she stood there. She began to focus as she watched the man who had caused her so much pain struggle to come to terms with his current reality. Then as the voice of an approaching nurse caught her ear, she quickly placed her gun back into her pocketbook and rushed from the room.

Face jumped from his seat and looked over at his mother. Pamela, in her healing but still fragile state, rested so peacefully as if the entire shooting had never taken place. Face placed his hand underneath his button-down Polo shirt. He tried to tear away the bullet-proof vest that felt like it had caved into his chest. He had been wearing the vest for the last few weeks because the attempt on his mother's life made it clear that he too was a target.

After taking several deep breaths and coming to terms that someone wanted him dead Face cautiously made his way towards the door to see where the woman had gone. He saw two female nurses walking towards him and he asked, "Did y'all see a young lady running down the hallway?" The shorter nurse with the dimple in her left cheek said, "Yes, she ran past us and went down the stairs. Is everything okay?" He paused for a moment and then said, " Do you know what she had on?" The other nurse smiled at him and said, "Sure. She was wearing white scrubs. White uniforms are my favorite. She was in a hurry but is everything okay?"

Face looked at the women and smiled before saying, "Yes, we good. Thanks." The ladies began to go on about their business as Face rushed back into the room with his mother. He pulled out his cellphone and dialed a number. The man answered on the first ring.

"What's up boss?"

"Kyle, are you still parked across the street?"

"Yes, I'm posted up. You good?"

"No. Somebody just tried to kill me!"

"What," Kyle shouted into the phone, as he pushed away the woman's head who was sucking his dick.

"Yo, you gotta go," he said, as he reached in his pocket and gave her fifty dollars before rushing her out of his car.

"I'm on my way up now boss."

"No, stay there. I need you to watch the front door and see if she comes out. She's young, light skinned with long black hair, and she's very attractive.
She's wearing a white nurse's uniform. Those scrubs."

As Face description of his assassin made his way into the phone, Kyle quickly noticed a young woman rushing out of the hospital's doors.

"Yo, I see her right now. She's in all white and she just jumped into a Yellow-Cab!"

"Follow her and find out where she lives or where she's going," Face ordered.

Once the line went dead, Kyle started up his car and made a quick U-turn onto Broad Street. Within moments he was in one car's reach of the cab. He noticed that the young woman had taken notice of him. Arianna continued to look back at Kyle as the driver drove to her requested destination. She pleaded with the cabbie to drive quicker as she told him they were being followed. Initially, the cab driver ignored her until she pulled out a hundred dollar bill and said he could have it-in addition to the fare-if he got away from the car she felt was in pursuit of her.

Kyle was close on her heels as luck turned in favor for Adrianna. As they both approached a yellow light, Arianna demanded the cab driver make the light. As he sped through, Kyle was right behind them and ready to follow suit until he noticed a police officer was right on his heels. Rather than risk being pulled over by the police, he grabbed his phone and input the cab's driver's license onto his notepad.

That one light had now placed him out of reach of Arianna. The pressure of the cops being behind him had slowed him down significantly because he had major heat in his car. So as soon as he could turn off without seeming suspicious to the authorities he took that turn.

Face was in the hospital furious. He had come within inches of losing his life. His mother too could have been a target and without the shield of a bulletproof vest she would have stood no chance of survival. He paced the floor back and forth as he made calls to his top men to discuss his security. There was clearly a problem and someone was out to get him. He needed answers.

Face then heard a small voice cry out to him.

"Baby, are you okay," his mother whispered.

"Yes mom. I'm fine. Why don't you rest? We can talk later. I'll go get the doctor?"

"No Face, I'm fine. I'll rest but I just had a dream about you and DJ and Reese. Remember when you were little and playing on July 4th?"

Face had to smile. Just the fact that his mother was speaking to him and unaware of the incident which had just occurred, relieved him. He didn't want her to deal with any additional stress.

"I remember lighting the firecrackers and I could see your smile. Y'all were so happy and having so much fun," Pamela said, as the memories brought a bright smile upon her face.

"I remember mom. I remember," he said, as he began to comfort his mom by rubbing her hair with his right hand.

"That firecracker sound was so real. I could hear it but I couldn't respond. Then something pulled at me and I just woke up."

Face knew what she had heard had been no dream. He was speechless. The woman who had come to take his life had ignited his mother's life and brought her from out of her coma. It was a blessing in disguise but still a disaster. His mother had been in close proximity of an attempted plot against his life and he needed to find out who had been so close to ending his days above ground. He would deal with her accordingly. Even though her actions had unintentionally given him his mother back, she would still pay for trying to kill him.

Chapter 2
Twenty-Two Minutes Later

The Yellow Cab pulled up and parked in front of The Mansion apartment complex on City Line Avenue.
"Thanks Simon," Arianna said, as she passed the dark, heavyset cabbie a hundred-dollar bill.
"Anytime. Your father was alright with me. Plus he always looked out for me so if you need me again I'm just a call away."
"I appreciate that. Thanks again," Arianna said as she exited the car and closed the door.

Standing outside of the cab she took a deep breath as she began to relive the early events of her morning. She rushed inside of her brand new luxury apartment complex. It was filled with the finest furniture her money could buy. She had lots of money and didn't mind spending it. After her parents were murdered, Arianna and her brother Robbie shared a million dollar life insurance policy. They were the sole beneficiaries. However, even though she had money it didn't take away the pain and misery that invaded her soul.

As she sat on her plush white leather sofa, she struggled to get her composure because her mind was stuck on Face. Had she killed him? She didn't know. Would she be arrested? Had she really gotten away from the man who was chasing her? The answers to these questions she simply didn't know.

Two Weeks Earlier

Jasmine pulled up and doubled parked her car in front of Robbie's and Arianna's Center City condominium. Arianna and Jasmine had really enjoyed themselves on their short vacation down in Atlantic City. They had spent plenty of money shopping in the high-end stores inside of the Pier's Shops at Caesars; and they both lost plenty of dough on the crap tables. They had no luck at gambling but enjoyed eating, socializing with the other guests, and they drunk plenty as they partied it up at Harrah's by the Pool.

Arianna grabbed her luggage from out of the trunk and closed it. Then she said her goodbyes to her friend and Jasmine waved goodbye as she drove off. Walking up the steps she was eager to tell Robbie about her venture in Atlantic City. She pulled out her key and as she opened the door to their place, she yelled out, "Robbie! Hi, I'm home!" He didn't reply immediately but she knew he was home because his Mercedes was parked in front of the door.

"Robbie I'm home," she shouted again. She sat her luggage down and went to the refrigerator to get a cold water. "Robbie, wake up. You know I have to tell you about all the fun I had down there." Arianna walked down the hall towards Robbie's bedroom. When she opened his door she noticed he was lying under the covers. The room was dark and all the curtains were shut. "Boy, wake up! I've been calling for you and you're in her knocked out," she said as she sat on the edge of the bed. "I know you can hear me so stop playing. You're gonna to listen to me. Who else can I talk to," Arianna said jokingly, as she laughed at her brother who was playing possum.

Then she noticed the wretched odor coming from the bedroom. "Robbie, what the hell is that smell," she yelled, as she pulled back the covers. "Oh God what the hell!" Arianna could not believe her eyes. Her body was numb. Her eyes had to be deceiving her. Under the heavy, navy comforter her brother's body was mangled. A huge chunk of his brain was gone and there was this gaping hole in his chest. It was like a sink hole and seeing his heartless chest reminded her of her father, Hood.

Arianna screamed to the top of her lungs. She began to hyperventilate. She ran from the room as vomit raced up from her stomach. She was running in circles. Screaming and purging up her pain. She was in agony and lost. This was her brother and her best friend. He was all she had left in the world and now she was alone. She yelled some more and her body began to tremble. She could not control her emotions as she felt her body fall to the floor. Her eyes felt like they began to jump out of her body and she fought to keep them open as a powerful force overcame her body and shut all her systems down.

Moments later, Arianna opened up her eyes and sat on the sofa. She was dazed, she was sick, and clearly shaken up. The blood on her hands ensured her she had not been dreaming. She knew if she walked back into her brother's bedroom he would still be laying on those bloody sheets, with several parts of his body missing.

Arianna needed to get her mind together. She didn't have anyone to talk with. Everyone she had trusted was no longer living on earth. She walked into the bathroom and removed her clothes. Robotically, she turned on the water and stood in the tub to take a shower. As the water struck her body she felt like she was being beaten. She fell down into the tub and wrapped her arms around her legs and began a serious of emotional breakdowns. She didn't know what to do. She was in a tub of water while her brother's putrid corpse lay in his bed.

Hahnemann University Hospital

Reese, Quincy, and Kyle were all standing guard outside of Pam's hospital room. Face had other members of his crew placed at all the exits and entryways of the hospital. Each man was armed and ready to kill anyone who looked like they posed a threat to Face or his mother. It was like the S.W.A.T. team had the hospital surrounded but this wasn't that type of team. This was a group of organized killers and they were cold blooded. They were loyal to their boss and would kill or be killed if that's what the situation called for.

"What the fuck happened man," Reese whispered. "Some crazy bitch snuck up in here and tried to kill me," Face said, showing Reese the bullet that was lodged into his bullet proof vest. "Damn man. You're lucky as fuck. Very fuckin lucky," Quincy said, shaking his head in disbelief and amazement because the bullet had penetrated the vest deeper than any of them had thought. It was truly a close call. "We gotta get to the bottom of this shit real quick. Can't have no loose end out here on these streets. People think they can pull a move like this but they got the game fucked up," Reese said. "Well I got that cabbie's license plate number. If she's got ties to him we'll find that out quick," Kyle said. "Find out everything y'all can about him. How long he's been working there, if he knows her, everything," Face demanded. "No worries. I'm on it," Quincy said.

Face looked at his three most loyal men and said, "From now on we all have to be extra careful. There's too many enemies lurking around, and plotting and scheming on us. We have to be out here watching the watchers and staying two steps ahead of these haters." Everyone nodded in unison as Face continued. "Y'all can leave for now but keep those men on those doors. I'm going to call a meeting in the next few days but right now I have to focus on getting my mom out of here. She won't be in here tomorrow I know that for sure. She ain't gonna be no sitting duck. I'm taking her home with me because that way I'll know she'll be alright."

Face gave each man a fist-pound before he walked back into the room to be with his sleeping mother.

Arianna was devastated. She was alone. There was no one left to talk to and no one she could confide in. She was empty. Her parents, Uncle Ron Perry and her favorite person in the world, her brother Robbie, were all dead.

Each day that passed brought up a new fear. She sat in the apartment waiting for the cops to come. She thought about what she would do if they knocked on the door. She didn't want to rot in jail for a crime she felt was justified. Face was the monster that had ended a generation of her family and a jail cell would not be her final destination. She thought about suicide. The comforts of taking a shitload of pills to end her misery seemed like a more suiting fix, but she cowered each time her body led her to the medicine cabinet.

Arianna's mind was playing tricks on her. She would see her father and Robbie, and she made a promise to them to live and carry on their legacy. Then her mother would appear and beg her to kill herself so she they could be reunited. She didn't know what was real or fiction anymore. She was out of her mind.

Arianna walked into her bathroom to get something to calm her. As she glanced into the mirror she screamed at the woman she had become. The image in the mirror was not the beautiful young woman she once was. She saw flashes of red and terror filled eyes, and along with the pain that embodied her face, it was a frightening sight. She quickly flung open the medicine cabinet and grabbed a small brown container. The pills she clutched in her hands were prescribed to her by her therapist. She held the Zoloft and knew she needed to get them into her system so she could think clearly. She was seeing things, hearing voices, as well as responding back to them.

Arianna took her pills and made her way back into the living room. Her fireplace was burning and as she sat on the floor, Indian-style, she swallowed three of the pills and chased them down with a large glass of pink Moscato. For now they were the only remedy. She needed to rest and as the bubbly drink continued to slide down her throat, she felt the familiar buzz of her concoction began to overtake her body.

Chapter 3
February 18th
Two Months Later

Inside his West Philly row-home the sounds of passionate moans flowed from Doc's bedroom. In the late hours of the night Doc had Marabella's naked body bent over his bed. Her hands were cuffed behind her back and Doc stood behind her as his hands tightly gripped Marabella's hips. With a deranged look on his face, Doc repeatedly thrust himself into his lover. For two weeks he had been enjoying many of his strange and weird sexual fantasies with his female creation. She was all his. He had made her just for himself and he was never going to let her go.

"Ahhh," she moaned, as Doc rammed his dick deeper inside of her newly sculpted pussy. As he looked down on the bed and saw a speckle of blood, he was turned on even more. Marabella had Doc hooked. He was highly infatuated with what he had created and when he was inside of her, he felt whole.

Doc no longer connected Marabella to what he once was. She was no longer a man. No resemblance of his former self existed. Peter was gone. Marabella was now all woman and the only woman Doc wanted. Doc had went on the internet and purchased a fake marriage license and he even preformed his own wedding ceremony. He brought Marabella a beautiful wedding ring and engraved, *The two of us until the end*, on both of their rings.

"I love you Marabella! I love you so much," he shouted out as he continued to penetrate her. Marabella didn't respond to Doc's love calls. The only sounds she made were of pain which filled the air.

Villanova, PA

Tasha and Veronica watched in amazement as Pamela jogged on the treadmill. Face had gotten his mother the absolute best physical therapy and she appeared to be beating all the odds. She was in tip-top health and it was quite a site to see her up and going, especially since it had only been a few months since she was on the brink of death. Pam didn't speak of the incident that almost ended her life. To cope she did what she always had when bad things happened in her life; she buried them deep and kept them there.

"Damn girl, you're in better shape than me," Veronica said. "Me too. You look real good," Tasha added. "Y'all two need to stop it," she said, as she wiped her sweaty forehead with her towel. "Shit, I ain't playing. I need to get my butt back on track. I've had one too many glazed doughnuts," Veronica said, as the trio began to laugh.

As Pamela's treadmill session ended, the three ladies exited the home gym and went upstairs. They watched as Face walked down the stairs and headed towards the front door. He had an early morning meeting with several members of his team and was rushing out the door. When he noticed the women, he kissed his mom and Veronica on the check, and then embraced his wife. He loved seeing these ladies happy and healthy. It made him feel like he was doing his job as a man. As his wife began to kiss him, he felt his son Norman III tug at his pants.

Face kneeled down beside his son and said, "What's wrong?" He could tell when something was bothering him. "Nothing Dad." Face wasn't buying it. "Norman what's up with the sad face," Face asked, as Norman III tried to avoid direct eye contact with his father. “Man, I’m not going to ask you again. Now don’t lie to me,” Face said. “Dad, I don’t like school.” Face smiled. “School? Why don’t you like school?” Norman III looked at his dad and said, “I don’t like my teacher. I used to like it before we got a new teacher.”

Face loved listening to his children and respected their opinions but he knew at the end of the day they were going to be educated. There was no way they were as wealthy as they were and his children were not going to have the best education possible. “Listen son, school’s not that bad. You’re going to be a doctor or a lawyer so you need to be in school. It will get better I promise,” Face said. “It’s not the school dad, it’s my teacher. He’s, he’s mean to me,” Norman said sadly. “Mean? What’s this mean stuff? Tasha, I need you to talk to my boy and find out what’s going on. Little man, I’m on it as soon as I get back home. I have a meeting to run to, okay,” Face said. “Okay dad,” Norman said, feeling a little better that he had told his dad about his new teacher. “I love you baby. I’ll be back,” Face said to his wife.

Face kissed his son on his forehead and he rushed out of the door. He jumped into his new tinted black Bentley Flying Spur and sped off. Tasha began to worry about their son. She had never heard Norman III say he was having difficulties with his teacher and she wanted to get to the bottom of things. Veronica told Pamela to walk her back down to the gym so she could put in a few minutes on the elliptical, giving Tasha and Norman III some privacy.

Tasha sat her son down on the couch in the living room. She gave him a huge hug before delving into the problem. “What’s wrong baby,” she asked, now noticing that for a few days he had been behaving a bit strangely.

She felt awful that she had not seen a change in him before but she was ready to fix things now.

Norman III sat with his head down for a minute before leaning over and whispering in his mother's ears. A look of shock splashed upon Tasha's face. Suddenly tears began to well up in her eyes as the words of her son made her ache.

"Did you tell anyone else," Tasha asked, as she wrapped her baby closely in her arms. "No; just you mommy," he said, as he hugged her tightly like he would never let her go. "Come on, go get your coat," Tasha instructed her son. She rushed towards the gym and told Pamela and Veronica she would be right back. Then she rushed back upstairs to her son and grabbed her coat out of the closet. Without delay, she and Norman III rushed inside of her S500 Mercedes and headed straight towards Bryn Mawr Hospital.

10:05 A.M.
Washington, D.C.

At a secret location, just a few blocks away from the White House, six high ranking members of the C.O.U.P. were all seated inside of a large boardroom. At the head of the table was The Vice President of the United States, Charles M. Bush. Directly to his right was Paul Warner. Charles Bush stood up and looked around the table at each individual.

"The President is not cooperating and does not want any association with this matter. I've tried to convince him that helping us eliminate these problems will be beneficial to us all and the people of the United States of America, but still he refuses," Charles Bush said. "The hell with that nigga," one of the men shouted, "he's not one of us anyway," he continued. "Calm down Senator," The Vice President said. "He's right. The President is becoming a problem for us and not with just this issue, but with so much more," a short, husky Caucasian man said. "We can eliminate him too. Just like we did Kennedy. We can make it look like an accident if we have to but he needs to go," another member said. "No," Charles yelled. "The President is a problem but he's okay for now. He's still controllable and we need him because the country needs him. Our priorities are of those names that sit in front of us. Robert Fuentes, the Russian Semion Mogilevich, South African radical, Victor Mutumbo, Internet billionaire, Harry Klien, Norman "Face" Smith Jr. and the few others there. That's were our focus must be.

Chapter 4
Later That Afternoon
Germantown
Philadelphia, PA

A block away from the Germantown Masjid, Face and his high ranking members of his organization sat around at a table talking. They were all comfortable in this location because it had been checked for bugs and any other recordings or unknown surveillance devices. This was just one of the many safe houses Face had situated around the country.

Everyone had been informed about the attempted murder on Face's life and he had someone looking into that; as well as other pressing matters. As they conversed Face knew he had other problems brewing and he had to tackle them without delay. He stood up to address his crew.

"My sources have told me something very serious and troubling. This is a big problem that's going to soon show its hand and we need to be ready. There is a secret organization of very powerful women and men called the C.O.U.P."

"The what," Frank "Underworld" Simms asked.

"The Committee of Unlimited Power. They are some of the most powerful and wealthiest people in the world. This group of individuals is responsible for the murders of Presidents, Judges, dictators, and even people close to you like Drug Kingpins."

Everyone at the table became highly tuned in when Face mentioned the latter of the group.

"So what are we gonna do about them," Frank "Underworld" Simms said. "We are going to continue doing what we do but with extreme caution. I have my people on it right now finding out everything that they can. When I learn more, their weakness and exactly what they want, I'll hold another meeting.

Frank make sure you do a thorough check on all the employees at your record label. It's becoming real popular and I don't trust anyone. The rest of you should take a second look into everyone who's around you. Something don't sit right, it ain't right. You might never get a second chance to make things right so don't slip. Don't let a love one or those so called friends be your demise, shit is real out here. We all have firsthand experience with informants and snitches. They are lurking and looking for your weaknesses to come up off of you. Don't give them that opportunity to turn a deal and get a reward off of your head."

When the meeting ended, Face, Reese, and Quincy got into an old Buick LeSabre and drove off. A few blocks away the car drove into a large gated car shop near Chew Avenue. "Y'all cars are ready," a short dark skinned man said. He had the biggest smile on his face because he was pleased to have been chosen to detail their cars. He knew who the crew was and their business meant good money, and lots more of it if they were satisfied.

As the trio walked into the back of the shop, Quincy checked out all their cars and paid the man five-hundred dollars for the detail. The man handed him their keys as he continued to thank them for their business. Each man was headed in a separate direction so as soon as they said their goodbyes they left.

Face wanted to get a slice of pizza from off of Erie Avenue so he headed towards the Ave. As he pulled to a red light he thought about how the game had changed. It was no longer the same game when Reese and he had started out. So many players were now dead and gone. He had watched the government take down some of the biggest drug dealers in America. John Gotti, Freeway Ricky Ross, Aaron Jones, and Big Meech were just a few on the list. Face began to wonder if he was lucky. He had beaten the government at trial but he knew that the fight was not going to be over just yet. Face didn't want to quit the game though; it was a part of him. He was great at what he did but he also knew that people wanted his head.

As he drove contemplating his next moves, he quickly pulled over and parked in an empty parking spot on 12th and Erie Avenue. In the privacy of his car he closed his eyes and said a silent prayer.

"*God forgive me for all my sins. I'm not sure why I am who I am or why I do what I do, but I know I'm not evil. You've put some great people in my life and I pray most that you protect my family. My mom, my wife and my children are my everything and they deserve your protection more than me. If I ever have to be sacrificed for them please don't hesitate to take me. Please protect me from the things I can't see and I beg you to bring my enemies out of hiding. Show their hand so I may know how to make my next move. Amen.*"

Face opened his eyes and began to pull out of the parking spot. He had two meetings left for the day and wanted to pick up that slice of pizza before he got so caught up that he forgot to eat something. Then as soon as he got in front of the store he saw one of his phones going off. It was a text message from Tasha that read:

Baby I need to talk to you when you get home. It's about our son and I don't want to talk over the phone. I'll talk to you when you get in. Love you

Chapter 5
West Philadelphia

Doc and Marabella were sitting in the kitchen across the table from one another. Doc had prepared chicken, rice, and mixed vegetables for dinner; and he brought out a sweet glass of red wine. Marabella was dressed in a pink nighty and her plush and perfectly rounded breast were on full display; and Doc wouldn't have it any other way. He loved seeing her body and each night it was mandatory that she wear a new, revealing piece of lingerie. He had purchased so many sexy outfits that she would never run out, or have to repeat one for at least a year.

"What's wrong," Doc asked, as he noticed his Marabella looked disturbed. She didn't respond. "Tell me what's wrong, don't ignore me and don't lie. I don't like that," he yelled. Marabella sipped on her wine and then looked Doc straight into his eyes. "Can you please release me and change me back," she pleaded. "I have money that no one knows about and I'll give it to you. I'll give you every dime if you will let me go," she said tearfully.

Doc stood up from his chair and walked around the table. He stood behind Marabella and placed his arms around her. He fondled her breast and then he leaned down and put his mouth to her ear. "I will never release you my love. You are my Marabella. My wife. There is no amount of money that could convince me to let go of you. Now stop all this crazy talk and finish your dinner. Tonight is going to be a special night. I got a new dildo to accompany us to bed this evening. This should be lots of fun."

Doc grinned as he walked back over to his seat and sat in his chair. The look on Marabella's face was stoic because there was nothing she could do. Doc had the entire house monitored with security cameras and rigged with booby traps. Marabella could not escape on her own, unless she was willing to risk bodily injury and possibly losing her life. And in the miraculous event she did get away it would only be for a moment. Doc knew Face would have his men looking all over for her, and he would go to great extremes to bring Marabella back.

Marabella was his slave. She had no free will and he was not looking to award her any freedoms. She was his prized possession and for now all Marabella could do was comply with what the doctor ordered; even if that meant exploring all of his demented sexual desires and acts. This was Doc's world.

8:15 P.M.
Los Angeles, CA

Inside a large gated warehouse over twenty workers were inside stacking and placing packages of some of the best marijuana in the world on shelves. The warehouse was heavily guarded by ten armed guards, each holding automatic weapons to protect the five ton shipment that had just arrived by way of Mexico.

Hidden in the grass that surrounded the warehouse was Paul Warner; who was dressed in camouflage gear from head to toe. His Remington 700 Rifle lay closely next to him as he looked through his night vision binoculars. After his early morning meeting with the C.O.U.P. he jumped on a private jet and headed to the west coast. Going on missions to kill people was his life. It gave him an adrenalin rush like nothing else could.

He sank lower into the grass as he spotted his target. The large man of Latin decent was next on the list.

Fernando Vasquez was dressed in an all-white Adidas sweat suit and as Paul sank lower in the grass he picked up his rifle. He took a few deep breaths as he controlled his breathing to relax his anxiety. The biggest marijuana dealer was about to meet his end. As Paul looked through his scope and the target's head lined up perfectly in the cross-hairs, he fired.

The mercury-tip slugged entered Fernando's head, exploding it and sending thousands of tiny pieces of his brain flying into the air. His security team rushed over to help him but his death was immediate.

Paul Warner had already packed up and moved on by the time the security had made their way towards Fernando. He was no armature. He had over two hundred hits under his belt and had traveled over four continents to get his targets. As he headed back to the east coast to get his next mission, he allowed himself to enjoy the rush that flowed through his body. He was the best at what he did and even with one arm; Paul Warner was, if not the best, one of the best assassins in the world.

Chapter 6
Later That Night
Villanova, PA

The entire house was tranquil and peaceful. After Face had gotten out of the shower he put on his black Polo robe and matching slippers and went to check on his children. Both Lil Norman and Suri were sound asleep. After a busy day of meetings and making moves throughout Philly, Face was simply happy to make it home safely to his family.

When he reentered his bedroom, he saw his wife sitting on the edge of the bed. She had been waiting on him so they could talk about Lil Norman. He noticed her facial expression and immediately he became concerned. Tasha never worried unless something was really wrong and her face clearly told the story before her mouth did.

Face sat next to his wife and looked into her eyes. "Baby, what's wrong. You've been crying and I'm not feeling how you're looking right now. What's up," he asked. She tried to speak but the words did not come out easily. He held her and tried to assure her that everything was okay. "Tasha you don't have to worry about me. I'm being careful, I swear."

Tasha was more afraid about what would happen when her voice gave life to the words she had to speak to her husband. They had been through some tough experiences but what she was about to tell him could be the death of him. "Face, our son's teacher touched him."

Face took a minute to hear the words that had just disgusted him and sent him into an instant rage. "What the fuck did you just say," he shouted. "Norman told me today that Father Jenkins has been touching his penis for the past few weeks." Face stood up and his hands trembled. He wanted to kill Father Jenkins. "Why didn't he tell me, why didn't you call my phone earlier Tasha," he yelled, as he began to pace the room. "I wanted to tell you but I needed to tell you at home. I didn't want to tell you this while you were on the streets," she said, as she struggled to keep herself from chocking on her tears.

"That's my son Tasha! That's my fuckin son Tasha! That's my boy," he screamed, as he fell onto his knees. "Why didn't he tell me? Don't he know I'll kill for him," he cried out. "He was too scared to say anything. Father Jenkins said he'd get you into trouble and they'd have to leave the school if Norman said anything."

Face felt like his heart was bleeding and all the veins inside of him were tying themselves in knots and cutting off his air supply. There were only a few times Tasha had seen her husband in a bad space, and even less times had she witnessed him cry; but today he had totally lost control of all emotional barriers. He ached and he bled with pain at the thoughts of what the Father had done to his son. Tasha did her best to comfort him but he was inconsolable.

"I took Norman to the hospital today and the doctors said physically he is fine. There were no signs of penetration…" Face immediately stopped her. "I don't want to hear that right now. I just can't. I'm going to kill him! It don't matter how he touched him! Don't nobody put their fuckin hands on my boy!!!"

Tasha knew Face was beyond words with his anger and she wanted Father Jenkins dealt with as well, but not if she had to lose her husband behind it. "The school is aware of what happened. I spoke with the authorities today at the school. He was under investigation and there were some complaints but nothing had stuck before. But he is going to jail for what he did to our child," Tasha cried out, as she began to feel the pain pour down upon her while she knelt down next to her husband.

"He's going to pay for what he did. Jail is not the kind of punishment I have in mind. I want him to suffer and that's what he's going to do for fuckin with mines," Face said as he stood up and helped his wife up. Face held his wife tightly in his arms as he gained some of his composure back. "Tasha, go lay down. I need to take care of some things," he demanded. "Face, baby what are you going to do," she pleaded. "Some things you just don't question Tasha. I've always been a man first. Let me do what I have to," Face said, as she sat on the bed and began to cry softly.

Tasha was afraid because she knew what he was capable of. Face always said that he hated cops, snitches and most of all child molesters. He said there was no jail on earth that should house them. They take a life of a child when they snatch away their innocence and the penalty for that should be their death.

Face looked at his wife and he knew she was hurting. He knew they both had anger and pain racing through them. He walked back towards her and hugged her tightly. "Trust me Tasha. I love you. You are my family and I'm going to protect you," he said, as he kissed her on the forehead and walked out of the room.

He quickly walked down the hallway and entered Lil Norman's bedroom. He watched his son as he slept peacefully. His blood began to boil because he felt as if he hadn't protected his son. He didn't see the signs and now the anger he felt for Father Jenkins was coming off his face like steam from a boiling pot. His tears fell and cut his skin with their rage.

Face walked over to his son and got in bed with him. His son, still halfway asleep, looked over at his dad and smiled slightly, before quickly dosing back off. Face wrapped his arms tightly around his son and told him he loved him. He repeated himself over and over again; as he hugged Lil Norman and swore that he'd never let anyone hurt him again. He pledged his love and vowed safety to his baby boy. For hours he lay with his son as his soul ached. Tonight he just needed his boy to know his father was there.

Chapter 7
Two Weeks Later

Inside a private suite in the Hilton Hotel, Quincy firmly had his lover Karen Brown, an F.B.I. employee, bent over the king-sized bed. As he fucked her hard, rough and rigid from behind, she allowed her loud moans of ecstasy to escape throughout the suite.

"Whose pussy is this bitch," he yelled out. "It's yours Daddy! All yours Quincy," she screamed as he continued to fuck her pussy harder. He used every muscle in his toned chocolate body to beat up her pussy and she loved it. She had cum so much that after her fifth orgasms her legs were numb and she couldn't feel her toes. Once again Karen was lost in her private world of complete bliss and she never wanted to leave.

Quincy had become her puppet master and there was nothing this woman wouldn't do for him. If there was information that came through the agency that she thought would be beneficial to him she didn't hesitate to forward it over. For over a year she had been giving him confidential information and she was fully aware of the consequences she would face if she was caught; but that didn't stop her from giving her lover what he needed.

This inconspicuous woman would never fall on the Feds radar as a double agent. She was the personal secretary for James Conner, The F.B.I.'s director of the Northeastern Pennsylvania branch; and he not only trusted her but he didn't think she was smart enough to do anything that he didn't tell her to do.

After their midafternoon sex session, Quincy cleaned up and made his way out of the hotel through a back entrance and got into his car. Karen watched from the high-rise window as his car pulled out of the parking lot. She waited another half an hour, as she did so many other times, and then she left the suite. Thankfully, they never had to worry about checking in or out of the room because the suite was owned by the T& F Real Estate Agency. Face and Tasha had their own private place for family, clients, and friends to stay when needed. Even with the privacy of the unit, Quincy didn't want to take any chance of the two being seen together, so she waited for him to leave before she made her way to her car.

Once in her car, Karen crashed into the seats from exhaustion. She couldn't wait to get home and rest. She knew she needed to soak her body in a hot tub of water with some Epson salt, but if she hit the bed first she'd have to wait until her body had the strength to handle the maintenance.

Lower Merion, PA

Inside of his home, Father Jenkins was extremely frustrated as he looked down at his newly attached ankle bracelet. The house-arrest monitor had been a requirement of his bail. After his arrest and being indicted and charged with seven counts of child molestation, the Father's distinguished career was now tarnished and his reputation in the community was destroyed. His trial was a few months away and the ankle bracelet would have to be worn until then. Another condition of his bond was mandatory weekly reporting to a state hearing officer, which he hated; however it was mandatory so he followed the order.

Today as he got ready to leave his house to go in to see the hearing officer, he noticed a police car pull up behind him as he got into his blue Honda mini-van. He waited to see what they wanted. They quickly approached his door and asked him to get out of the car and he obliged their request.

"What's going on officers," he asked. "You're under arrest for violating the terms of your probation," one of the officers said. "How, I haven't left my house all week. There must be some mistake," he pleaded, as they placed him in handcuffs. "You can tell it to the judge but today we have to take you in," the other officer said.

Father Jenkins was irate. He was embarrassed also because his neighbor had looked out of her window and saw him being taken into custody. "You will be hearing from my lawyer. You are making a big mistake," he said. The officers ignored him and placed Father Jenkins into the back of their police car.

"This is absurd," Father Jenkins yelled as the officers got into the car. They continued to ignore him as they quickly sped off down the quiet street. Neither officer said a word as the Father protested his rearrests. Within fifteen minutes the patrol car pulled into a private driveway where a tinted black van was waiting. Two masked men were seated inside of the van.

The officers escorted Father Jenkins from the back of the squad car and over to the van. "What's going on? I demand some answers here," Father Jenkins shouted. Reese passed one of the Caucasians officers an oversized sealed envelope that was filled with twenty-thousand dollars. "We got it from here," Reese said, as the Father looked around dumbfounded. "Got what from where? What's going on son," Father Jenkins asked. "I'm not your fuckin son. You gotta problem with people's sons. That's your problem but we've got you covered."

Father Jenkins got quiet. He had heard some very quiet rumors about the powers of Norman "Face" Smith Jr., but nothing had ever been proven. Today he was going to learn about the powers of a boss. He was going to see how someone who thought they were untouchable and protected by the church would pay a price for messing with a King's son.

"Kyle let's go, Doc is waiting," Reese said, as he threw the Father in the van.

Chapter 8
T & F Real Estate Office
Downtown Philadelphia, PA

Tasha was inside of her office, typing at her computer, when a knock on her office door startled her. Her new assistant Amy opened the door and stuck her head inside. "Mrs. Smith, you have a visitor," she said. "Can you take their name and tell them I'll get in touch with them soon. I'm too busy right now," Tasha said, never taking her eyes away from her computer. "Mrs. Smith I think you need to take this meeting. It's a guy from the I.R.S. He said his name is Timothy Feeney."

Tasha speedily stopped typing and looked up at her new assistant. She rushed to get up and began to fix her clothes. "Okay, you can send him in." Moments later a short, heavyset, Caucasian man, dressed in a tight, dark blue suit walked into her office holding his briefcase.

"Hello Mrs. Smith. My name is Timothy Feeney and I'm a Federal Agent for the I.R.S.," he said, extending his hand for her to shake it. After shaking hands, she offered him a seat in one of her office chairs. "Nice meeting you Mr. Feeney. How can I help you," Tasha asked. "I'm here because we're going to do an audit on your company. It's very random. We just pick and your company has come up in our rounds of random audits," he said, with a slight grin on his face.

Tasha could smell his bullshit a mile away but was ready to play ball. "Oh, is that so," she said, as she smiled and stared directly through him. "Yes. We would like your full cooperation in this matter. We want to get started on Monday and we need all of your financial records to help this audit go fast and without a glitch," he said. "Oh great, I'll make sure you have everything you need. So glad we have accountants and all those types of people who can handle those things for your guys. You won't have any problems getting what you need. Monday, right," she said. "Yes, Monday. We'll be back to handle things. It was nice meeting you Mrs. Smith," he said as he stood. "Nice to meet you as well," Tasha said, as she shook his hand and escorted him out of the office.

Tasha knew something was off but wanted to make sure they were good on their end. She sent Face a text message:

Baby, I just got a surprise visit from the IRS. They want to do an audit on Monday.

Face quickly responded back:

No problem, we'll be good. I'll take care of it.
Love you

Quickly, Tasha called her accountant and financial advisors to alert them of the visit. Face had advised her many times that one day they would get an audit. It was no surprise to her but she wanted to be ready for it. Everything would be in order and there would be nothing for them to trace because her team knew how to make the money trail stick to the script. It would be clean and her company would prove to be legit.

Tasha took a moment to text Face back:

Where are you

Face Responded:

I'm with the Doc. I have to take care of this cold.

She knew exactly what her husband was talking about. Things in her home had been rocky and once this cold was cleared up, they would be able to get back to some sense of normalcy.

I.R.S. Agent Timothy Feeney walked out of the T & F Real Estate Agency office building and got inside of the backseat of a waiting hunter green Ford Taurus. Paul Warner was in the back waiting on him.

"How did it go," Paul asked. "It went well. She seems very nice and eager to comply," Timothy said. "I don't care if she seems nice. We are here on business," he yelled. "Okay, I understand. Well our audit will begin on Monday as planned. We will do our job. My agents are great at their job and if money has been mismanaged or misappropriated, we will know it. Any corruption or misleading will be found; I can promise you that," he said. "Great, that's what I want to hear," Paul said.

Timothy Feeney was a man of the law but he was concerned as to why Paul Warner had taken notice of the T & F Real Estate Agency. Their records with the I.R.S. were clear and the company paid their taxes when due. "Mr. Warner, I just have to ask why you are so concerned with this company. They don't owe us any money that I can see and I wouldn't want to waste my agents' time on a silly fishing expedition," Timothy said. Paul Warner moved closer to Timothy and grabbed him by the collar. "You listen to me, I don't care what you haven't seen before because I know what you're not seeing is there. You have to look and find the missing and stop asking me so many damn questions. I don't fish my friend, I catch. So just do your job and get your best agents to find what I'm looking for," he demanded, as he let go of Timothy.

Mr. Feeney was afraid. His clammed up and didn't want to make direct eye contact with Paul Warner. He had heard about his reputation and now that he had seen a glimpse of it in action, he was frightened and wanted to get this task over as quickly as possible.

Timothy kept his head lowered as the driver drove them to his destination and just agreed with everything else Paul Warner said until he got there. Once he exited the car he noticed he had a wet spot on his pants. He was so afraid of Paul that he had peed himself.

Mount Laurel Private Cemetery

Arianna parked and slowly got out of her Audi Q7 truck. Her fitted chinchilla kept her warm and protected against the cold and blistering winds. As she walked down the dusty pathway that led to her family's burial site, she paused for a brief minute. She continued on as the wind reminded her of how cold of a day it was; so she walked up on the burial plot and looked at the three tombstones.

Seeing the graves of her father, mother, and brother was overwhelming. It was the worst feeling in the world to stand in front of the graves as she realized she was left out in the world alone. She yelled out, "Daddy I need you here! I'm all alone and I need you to protect me." The tears dropped from her eyes as she continued, "God why would you take them all from me?"

She stared at her father's tombstone as if she was waiting for a response. Truth is, she wanted him to say something to her. She wanted to hear anyone of their voices. Yet, the only noises she heard were that of the wind and the squirrel who rummaged the trees for nuts. She sat on the cold ground and sang a song that had been playing in her car before she got to cemetery. The lyrics of *It's So Hard To Say Goodbye* by Boys II Men came from her soul and as the words penetrated the cold air, her body broke down.

It hadn't been too long ago that she had to come out of her state of denial and call the cops to report her brother's murder. The detectives were all over her story and although she had an iron clad alibi and no motive to kill her brother, they still had to look deeper into her as a possible suspect because she waited four days before calling in the murder.

The house had the worst stench imaginable but still she didn't want to call authorities. She knew the moment she dialed the number she had to admit that Robbie was gone. She walked to his bedroom and looked at his corpse, and then she sat back on the living room floor and drank her wine and took her pills. She was in and out of consciousness and remembers seeing her mother's face. She could hear her mother telling her, "Arianna, he's gone. He's with us now." That's when she knew she needed to make the call.

Chapter 9
West Philadelphia

Father Jenkins had never known fear like he was experiencing now. Naked and strapped onto a long, cold metal table, Father Jenkins knew he could not pray his way out of this. Doc stood only a few feet away from Father Jenkins as he licked his lips with anticipation. Doc couldn't wait to experiment on his new catch. He had lots more toys and gadgets to test and his hands began to sweat as he grew eager to explore.

Face and Reese were inside of the basement with them but neither had said a word. Face was so angry he had to talk himself down because he knew he wanted to kill Father Jenkins immediately; but that would prove faulty since he wanted the man that hurt his son to suffer. Face gathered himself and then made his way over to the petrified Father Jenkins.

"You know why you're here and I know why I'm here, but I don't know what I want done to you," Face said. "No, I don't know why I am here! I haven't done anything," Father Jenkins cried out. "My name is Norman "Face" Smith Jr. and my son," Face paused for a moment before continuing. "Lil Norman is my son." The Father's eyes almost popped out of his head when he realized exactly who Face was. "You're Face," he asked. "Yes, I'm Face you low-life son of a bitch. You must be one sick fuck, touching kids though," he replied. "No, I didn't touch…"

Face started choking Father Jenkins in mid-sentence until he began to lose color. Reese and Doc struggled but they finally were able to remove Face's hands from around Father Jenkins' neck.

"Please, please, please. I didn't do anything," Father Jenkins softly cried out. His windpipe was weak and he was scared shitless, literally. Face approached Father Jenkins and the scared man tensed up again, but Face didn't touch him.

"My son means everything to me and I'd never let anyone get away with what you did to him. You're supposed to be a man of God but you're nothing more than a fuckin pedophile faggot," Face screamed. "Doc, take care of this motherfucker, he likes to touch boys," Face said, as he looked at Reese and walked out of the basement.

"I'm innocent, I swear," Father Jenkins cried out as he tried to plead with Reese and Doc. "Shut the fuck up. The verdicts in already," Reese said, as he walked over to the metal table. Doc and Reese unstrapped Father Jenkins and began to turn him onto his stomach. He tried to fight his way loose but it was useless. The small man was no match for the strength of Doc, let alone Reese. Once he was on his stomach, they strapped him back to the metal table in his new position. Reese made his way upstairs and when he came back downstairs there were four men who came back down with him.

Kyle had dropped off four crack addicts. They were promised one hundred dollars each if they participated in Doc's devious plan for his new victim. They were filthy and reeked of a stench filled with dirt, piss, booze, and god knows what else; but they were just what the doctor ordered.

Reese stood back on the wall as Doc stepped up to the plate. "I'm going to go first," he said, as he walked around to Father Jenkins and placed a small sock firmly in his mouth. He then attached a piece of gray duck tap to his mouth so the sock would not come out. Doc then sat the table straight up. It was already grounded into the floor and very sturdy. He walked directly behind Father Jenkins and began to fuck him in his shitty ass. Father Jenkins squirmed on the metal table but there was no way he wasn't going to get the full impact of the Doctor. He was strapped to a table and as Doc grabbed his ass cheeks and spread them further, as he ferociously rammed his dick into the Father. He screamed but was not heard by anyone who would save him.

Father Jenkins cried and as his tears made their way down his face, the train had begun to ensemble. The crack addicts all wanted their money and they knew they had to follow the leader. So like good employees they followed the orders of Doc. They each fucked the now bloody asshole of Father Jenkins as his body trembled and he begged for mercy. Each wanted to outshine the other, as if a tip would be included, and they went longer and harder into the virgin anus of Father Jenkins. Reese felt queasy as he watched the men ram their dicks into the Father but he stood watch because he knew it was what he deserved.

When Doc felt they had earned their pay, he turned the men over to Reese. Reese then took the men out of the back of the home to Kyle, who paid them for their services and dropped them off. Reese went back downstairs to talk to Doc and to thank him for being their when they needed him most. Doc was in all smiles as he looked over at Father Jenkins who lay slumped on the table like a Vegas whore. Doc was thankful to Face because now he had a new toy to play with. Doc walked Reese out and then quickly made his way back to Father Jenkins.

"Wake up Father," Doc said, as he poured a glass of ice cold water over his head. Father Jenkins began to squirm and tried to release himself. "Stop that stupid," those are metal chains and security straps. You are never going to wiggle your way loose," Doc said to him, as he removed the sock and tape from his mouth. "Now you've pissed off my good friends and that's why you are here. I'll do anything for those guys. Whatever they ask. I'll kill you if they want me to, but they haven't said what else they want me to do to you yet. I don't know how long I'm going to be able to keep you but I am going to enjoy you while you're here," Doc said, as he cut off the lights and made his way upstairs.

Father Jenkins didn't speak as he stood in the darkness. He didn't know what to say because he knew he was in the hands of a maniac. His anus was on fire and he could feel the blood dripping from his ass, as it ran down his legs and fell to the floor. He felt shame, he felt dirty, but he couldn't pray. He didn't know what to say to God. He had gotten to this place because of his inability to keep his hands off of little boys and maybe this was the punishment he deserved.

Chapter 10
Four Days Later

Tasha and her staff felt a bit uneasy as the I.R.S. agents prodded them. They were going through their files, looking at checks, and the rest of their financial records. Tasha was upset because she knew it wasn't an ordinary audit but she could not let her frustrations show. Agent Timothy Feeney walked around with a note pad in his hand as he wrote down continuous notes. Every so often he would excuse himself or step away and use his cellphone. Tasha knew something was up with him. He was behaving very suspiciously.

She sat at her desk and looked at the card that Agent Feeney had given her. She stared at him and her intuition was clear that he wasn't legit. "Something's not right," she whispered. She just felt it in her gut.

4th & Spring-Garden Streets

Face had his driver pull into the parking lot of the Rite-Aid Pharmacy. The tinted black Range Rover parked in the back, away from the other cars. Moments later a silver Honda Accord pulled up and parked beside them. Face watched as a short, skinny white man got of the car and walked up to the Range Rover. Face opened the backseat passenger door and the man got inside.

"What's up Vince, what did you find out," Face said, as he shook the man's hand. "You've got some serious problems on your hands," he replied. "Like what," Face said, solely tuned in to Vince's words. "I checked out the surveillance at Mike Conway's office and I do believe its Paul Warner. He's the man who killed Mike. He lost an arm but I see him moving like he still has both of them,"

Vince said. "Who is this Paul Warner dude, should I know him. I think his name has come up before," Face asked. "He's a paid assassin," Vince said, as he looked at Face. "He works for the United States Government and he's no joke. He's the best," Vince continued.

Face nodded his head as he sat there calmly and Vince told him more. "He's a master of military intelligence and has worked on many covert missions. Formally he was a navy seal. One of the elite members who traveled the globe and he was trained to kill. I also found out that he was a part of the assassination team that traveled to Cuba to kill Fidel Castor. This man is dangerous and he has a lot of major players behind the scenes who support him. He's a member of the C.O.U.P. too. It's a secret society and the things they've been able to get away with are endless and scandalous."

Face sat still as he absorbed the flood of information about Paul Warner. This was a lot to take in but he knew he needed to know everything that was going on around him. "So the C.O.U.P. is the real deal. I knew they existed," Face said, as he sat deeper into his seat. "Yes, they are the real deal. They've been around some time just like the Skull & Bones Society, and the Committee of 300 who basically run this world. George Bush is a member of the Skull and Bones Society and President Clinton and his wife Hillary are members of the Committee of 300. These organizations run deep and their history dates back to the early days. They have produced over fifteen presidents; they pop out senators, congressman, and generals all the time. They have even gotten a few United States Supreme Court Justices into power. The late Senator C.W. Watson was a C.O.U.P. man and Paul Warner was his right hand guy."

"How did you find this information," Face asked. "Research, hard core research. I have a few sources inside of D.C. and before Mike was murdered he had been secretly investigating Paul Warner and the C.O.U.P.'s organization. While he was investigating C.W. Watson for you, Paul Warner was a constant in that circle. Warner was inside of Watson's home when it blew up but somehow that guy got away," Vince said. "Do you know where Paul Warner is right now," Face asked. "Yes, he's somewhere in Philadelphia. You need to be careful. Don't just watch your back; watch everything and everybody around you. He doesn't care if you're with your wife or if he has to kill your children. He is a true cold blooded killer. It's not about money with this guy; he's in it for the love of the sport. That's what he calls murder, a blood sport. So be smart about the moves you make," Vince said.

"Vince, what else can I do," Face asked, feeling the heat because he knew Paul Warner was a serious threat to him and his family. "Don't get comfortable. Switch up your cars, your routine. Stay low and let see what else I can find. You have a problem with your government because they have a problem with you. You are no different than Castro, Saddam Hussein, Noriega, Freeway Rick Ross, or Pablo Escobar. They want you dead or locked away in a Federal prison until you come out in a box," Vince said. "Thanks Vince. It's not the best news I've had all day but it's the news I needed to hear. Keep getting information on the C.O.U.P. and on Warner. I'll take care of everything else," Face said, as he shook Vince's hand before he got out of the Range Rover.

Moments later Face rode in the back of his Range Rover down Spring Garden Street. He was silent and requested that no music be played. He was a thinker and he needed to do what he did best; come up with a master plan. This was a game of chess and he had to stay five steps ahead of his enemies. His mind began to get a bit cloudy as he thought about his son and the pain he had endured. He hadn't given himself the necessary time to grieve or deal with the situation, and at present he didn't have the time too. He was a born leader and he could handle pressure but the weight of his son's pain weighed heavy upon him.

As he refocused and thought of his options, his mind drifted to a time in his life when things were so different. There was less stress. There was time for fun and games, and he could just be free; no looking over his shoulders and worrying about people trying to kill him and his family. Things were so different back then…or so it seemed.

Chapter 11
Twenty-Two Years Earlier
Los Angeles, California

Face sat inside of the driver's seat of the Cadillac waiting for Mouse to come out of the house. Face had been waiting over an hour and now his nervousness and fear had shown up. This was the longest Mouse had ever taken and all the things that could have gone wrong started to play in Face's head. Just then Mouse calmly walked out of the house and got into the car.

"Man, what happened? You were in there forever," Face said. "Just had to take care of business, that's all," Mouse said. "You know sometimes niggas ain't right out here on these streets," Mouse continued. Even though Face was barely a teenager he knew the game. Besides his mom had taught him about the streets and said, "That life ain't pretty but sometimes we end up in the game. If you're gonna play in the dirt you better know what's in it."

"So did Calvin pay you," Face asked, as they started to drive away. "Yes, he had to make his payment in another way," Mouse said. "What do you mean," Face questioned. "He paid with his life," Mouse said, and Face eyes grew wider. "Listen here. When I tell you things you better never let them leave your lips," Mouse said as he looked directly at Face. "Calvin was working for the F.B.I. and he was a paid informant. So I did what everyone should do to a snitch, I offed him."

Face hated snitches. He didn't care what happened to him and at just ten years old he had learned that you never tell. It was not a loyal or respectful thing to do. "What did you to do him Mouse," Face asked, curious about how Calvin died. "I shot him twice in the head and I cut his fuckin tongue out," Mouse said as he went inside his jacket pocket and pulled out a zip lock bag that held Calvin's tongue inside of it.

"This is what you do to snitches. You take away their words for an entirety. You never rat and Lil Man on my life, I never wanna hear you was no bitch as snitch," he said heatedly. "No Mouse, I'd never do that. I promise Big Homey, I'll never snitch," Face said. "Good, keep it that way. We all make choices out here and sometimes you've gotta take a hit for what you chose but you don't bring nobody down on your shit. Don't be no coward out here and don't be weak for nobody. Always be a man. That's who you are."

Chapter 12
12:45 A.M.

It had been three months that Kyle and Quincy spent searching for the cab driver who led Arianna away from Hahnemann Hospital after she tried to kill Face. Finally they had a solid lead on him and needed to pay him a visit. On the corner of 27th Street and Grays Ferry Avenue, Kyle and Quincy sat inside of a black tinted van as they watched cab drivers come in and out of the large gated building. The building was the dispatch headquarters.

The man they were after was Simon Vdondo. He was an immigrant from Nigeria who was living in the U.S. on a temporary green card. They knew where he lived, how often he visited his girlfriend and the kind of car he drove. The car he drove was on the corner of 27th Street and when Simon went to open his car door he was greeted by Kyle, who had a loaded .357 pistol, pointed directly at his head.

Simon threw up his hands without hesitation. He had been robbed before and didn't want to make any false moves. However, when Kyle told him to walk towards the van Simon tried to take off running. Instantly, Quincy tackled him to the ground and knocked him across the head with his chrome piece. Then the men lifted Simon up and threw him in the van.

This had never happened to him before. He had been robbed and didn't mind if the men took the few dollars he had on him, or even his car but this was new. As he sat in the van neither man said as word. As Quincy sped off, Kyle kept his gun pointed at Simon. He was a small village man and had only come to America to get his piece of the pie. He had a wife and children back home to provide for and now everything was being compromised. He prayed to God and as he looked at the door handle, Kyle quickly yelled, “Don’t even think about it.” Simon didn’t want to die. He knew he had to follow their orders if there would be any chance of saving his life.

West Philadelphia

Doc was upstairs getting Marabella ready for bed while the guys waited downstairs. Face stood a few feet away from Father Jenkins’s mutilated, naked corpse and felt sick to his stomach at the site. Reese stood beside him with a big grin on his face because he was pleased to see that Father Jenkins got exactly what he deserved.

“Man Doc did a number on him,” Reese said as he looked at the corpse. “Yeah, this shit is crazy. My stomach is all messed up,” Face said, still trying to keep his food inside of his stomach. Doc came walking back downstairs. “Hey guys, I hope you like my work,” he said. “What did you do to this dude,” Reese asked. “I took good care of him. I cut his cock off. I didn’t want him to use it anymore. He didn’t know how to use it properly anyway and then I took my favorites out. You guys know how much I love my eyeballs. Just delicious,” Doc said, as Face gagged.

Reese was intrigued with Doc. He knew he was crazy but felt like he was cool at the same time. “Man I’m glad you’re on our side Doc,” Reese said. “What else did you do to him, he looks all torn apart,” Reese continued. “Well I’ve been eating him,” Doc said. “What,” Reese yelled. “Yeah, I’ve been eating him. If you look at his skull I’ve taken some of it and enjoyed a nice stew. Marabella had some too. I didn’t tell her what was in it but she enjoyed it.”

Reese fell to the floor laughing. He just couldn't get over Doc. "Doc, you eating niggas though. You a wild boy for sure." Doc smiled at Reese, and even Face had to laugh at how crazy Doc was. "Doc, how did he die," Face asked. "I ate him alive and he suffered. He probably went into cardiac arrest from all of the blood loss. I cut his tongue out. We ate that yesterday and I just kept cutting pieces off until he was done. He won't hurt anyone anymore Face, I made sure of that."

Face was pleased to hear that he suffered. He didn't care what Doc did to him but he had to suffer. That was his main priority. The pain Father Jenkins felt would never ease the pain that lasted in Face's heart, but it was a starting point to the healing process.

Reese handed Doc a payment of ten-thousand dollars and the two men made their way towards the door. Doc looked over at Reese and said, "You want to come back over for dinner, Reese?" Reese started cracking up and replied, "Yup Doc, you a wild boy!"

Chapter 13
16th Street & Allegheny Avenue

Kyle and Quincy had Simon's tied down to a wooden chair in a small row house. He had been beaten and tortured until he finally gave up all the information he knew about the young woman who had shot Face. At first he put up a fight but once they had pulled down his pants and started pinching his dick with toenail clippers, he gave up more information to them than when they were punching and kicking him in the face.

Simon was once a driver for the infamous drug Kingpin Hood, and the woman who wanted Face dead was named Arianna-who happened to be Hood's daughter. Simon just happened to be at the hospital that morning. He was paid to take her to her destination. He drove her to where she wanted to go. He had nothing else to do with Arianna. One could say he was just at the wrong place at the wrong time.

Quincy and Kyle stepped to a private area in the house and began discussing the fate of Simon. "So, what do you want me to do with him," Kyle asked. "He's seen our faces," Kyle continued. Quincy thought about it for a minute before responding. "I don't want to kill him. He's not our problem, she is." Kyle looked at Quincy harshly and said, "Kidnapping carries a thirty-year minimal and I'm not ever stepping foot back in no state jail. You getting soft or something because if you won't kill him I will."

Quincy gave what his friend said some thought but then responded, "Man, he's innocent. We are not going to kill him!" Kyle was heated. "Listen Q, if you don't kill him and this shit ever comes up, I'm going to hold court in the streets with your ass. This is your call but just know I'm not down with it. He saw us. He's supposed to die!"

Twenty minute later they pulled their van up to D Street and Erie Avenue. They pushed the now naked Simon out of the door and sped off into the darkness. Simon thanked God for sparing his life.

Two Days Later

After meeting with private investigator Vince Harris, Face relocated his entire family to another home that was owned by Face and Tasha; but was listed under an anonymous company. It was a beautiful place and Bala Cynwyd, PA. The house had six bedrooms and three bathrooms. It was spacious and came with a state of the art alarm and surveillance system, a pool, a small pond, and a three car garage. The street was private and you could not access the property without having access to the security gate.

Tasha asked her husband no questions about the move because she had full confidence in him. He wanted their family safe and couldn't take any chances with their lives. He hired armed guards to protect the grounds but he had a feeling that one day he would meet up with Paul Warner. One day very soon...

For two days Kyle had been secretly watching Arianna's every move. She had no idea she was being monitored as she made her daily routines with no worries of being tailed. He watched her at school, when she went to the bank, and as she jogged down Kelly Drive. Kyle had orders from Reese to kill her the first chance he got and although he had plenty of opportunities to grab her up and end her life; there was something about this young lady that kept him from completing his assignment. She was beautiful and Kyle wanted to know more about her. He knew her name but he wanted to know what she was about, why she had tried to kill Face; even though he knew Face was responsible for murdering her father, mother, and his brother. Her eyes lit up something inside of him that he knew couldn't grow, but still he wanted to know who Arianna Camile Jackson was.

Chapter 14

Paul Warner sat inside of the tinted black Chrysler 300 as he waited at a red light. For almost a month he had been secretly roaming the streets of Philadelphia. The only people who knew he was in the city were a few members of the local F.B.I and I.R.S. agencies. He was here on a personal mission and that was to kill. An enemy of the C.O.U.P. was surely an enemy of his. He wanted to take out his next target and ensure he left no clues that could tie the murder back to him or his secret society.

With the many skills Paul possessed, he had no problem adapting to the underworld in Philly. For over a year Paul had compiled info and studied all the major players on the east coast. He knew every Kingpin, corporate embezzler, and corrupt politician in Pennsylvania, New York, Boston, Washington D.C., Baltimore, Delaware, and in New Jersey.

So far his current target had escaped his immediate radar. He did not know where Face and his family were staying. They had managed to elude him and the local government for now. Paul knew Face was wealthy and connected so he would have to do some searching to get him back in his scope.

"Hopefully one day soon you'll slip up and I'll see you. I'd much rather end this sooner than later," he said softly, as he drove his car down Broad Street.

T& F Real Estate Agency

Tasha sat at her desk as she watched the I.R.S. agents pack up a few boxes before leaving out of the office. She watched from her office window as three of the agents got into their cars. Timothy Feeney was getting into a car to leave as well, and one of Tasha's employee's secretly wrote down the black Chrysler's 300 license plate number. As Tasha watched him talk to the man inside of the car, she found it very hard to read their body language or their lips because the car was tinted. Either way her gut was sending signals stronger than ever that the man in the car was no good. Now that she had a license plate number she would hand it over to Face. He would be able to find out some information and maybe put her suspicions to rest.

Cherry Hill, New Jersey

In the large parking lot of the Cherry Hill Mall, the silver BMW pulled in and parked. Face and Reese sat patiently and quietly inside of the car as the waited. Moments later a caramel brown Infiniti pulled up and parked directly beside them. Drug Kingpin Frank "Underworld" Simms and his right hand man, Craig, got out of the car. Face exited his vehicle and asked the two men to take a walk with him.

"What's up Face? What's the emergency," Underworld asked with a concerned look upon his face. Frank "Underworld" Simms was another powerful drug kingpin on the east coast. He was also the owner of Underworld Entertainment, which was a lucrative and successful record label. Face and he had become good acquaintance over the past year, and were introduced to one another by their wives.

"I have a serious problem on my hands that I have to deal with and it could get ugly. The last thing I want is you and your crew to get tied up in it," Face said. "Yo man, you don't need my help clearing up this problem," Underworld said, as they continued to walk through the parking lot. "No, I'll be okay. I gotta put a little distance between us so that you're cool to. This is a very serious problem and if I don't eliminate this issue it could be the downfall for all of us," Face continued. "Man, who is it? The Feds again," Underworld asked. "No, not this time. It's the people behind the Feds. They're the real puppet masters. They are pulling all kinds of strings and we have to be careful."Underworld nodded his head as he listened to the seriousness in Face's voice, and noticed the stern expression on his face.

"So what do you want me to do," Frank asked. "I need you to take a trip down Florida," Face said, as he handed him a card with a name and number on it. "Juan Carlos is a good friend of mine. He will take good care of you, shit he'll take better care of you actually with the prices he has set for you. He's a major distributor with straight ties to Columbia. He knows you're going to contact him so everything is set," Face said. "So our business is done," Underworld asked. "Yes, for now. Just take care of yourself and we'll talk again," Face said as the men shook hands and parted ways.

Underworld and Craig watched as Face got back into his car and pulled off with Reese.

"So what do you think about this Frank," his friend Craig asked. "I think that something's going on that's out of our hands and our reach. Face must have gotten wind of something heavy and now he has to pull back from some of the business he handles. He's a good man though. Man of his word and a straight shooter. I've got mad respect for him and I know men like him only come once in a lifetime."

Craig looked at Frank and said, "Well I got a real dude next to me right now. What we've got going is good. We just need to link up with this new connect and make our situation a whole lot better."

New York City

Inside of her lavish office located in Manhattan New York, Gloria Jones sat at her desk staring at two small pictures that were in her hands. One of the photos was of a Face, the man she never stopped loving; and in the other hand she held a photo of her son, Samaj. Face and Samaj shared many of the same features because in reality Face was her son's father. He was the son that Face and no one in his family knew of. The only person who knew about this little dark secret was Gloria's loving husband.

The last time she saw Face was when she represented him at his Federal drug trial. She knew that she was pregnant with his baby back when she was a college student in Philly. But things between the two were not meant to be. When she returned to New York on her college break, she hid her pregnancy from Face and never told him when she returned to Philly to represent him. It was a hard secret for her to carry and when she met back up with him during the court proceedings she wanted to spill her guts. She wanted to tell him how much they looked alike and even acted the same in many ways. She wanted to brag about how handsome Samaj was and how he had his father's eyes, but at the last moment she couldn't. She was afraid that he'd be angry or that he would deny their child.

Gloria was a powerful and well respected defense attorney in the state of New York. There wasn't a man or woman that could match her talents in a court of law; but there was one man who could bring her to her knees. Face had her heart and her heart had been heavy lately. As she looked at the picture of her now fourteen year old son, she thought of how her life could have been if things had worked out between her and her true love.

Chapter 15
6:19 A.M.
One Week Later

Kelly drive is a beautiful four mile path where many joggers, bike riders, and families come to visit. It runs along the Schuylkill River with rows of soaring trees and the view is very serene. Arianna found the drive to be a place where she could run and clear her mind; and the path was challenging as the trail provided hills for an incline and winding pathways.

This particular morning, Arianna awake very early and eager to get to Kelly drive. She wanted to get some clarity from all the disheartening thoughts that invaded her mind, so she put on her grey Nike jogging outfit and made her way towards the drive.

As she ran along the path she never noticed the man who had been following her. He had been watching her from the moment she stepped foot out of her car, until this very moment. His orders had been clear. She was the target and he needed to get to her quickly. She was alone and this would be the best time to complete his task.

The dark-skinned, husky man quickly approached the small framed woman and tackled her to the ground. She was completely caught off guard by her attacker and didn't scream initially because she was dazed and confused. Her mind had kicked in to the situation that she found herself in, and she started to fight the man off. He was heavy and very strong and she proved to be no match for him. She screamed and began to kick, punch him, and she tried to claw at his eyes; but nothing was working.

Suddenly, another man appeared and began to scuffle with her attacker. He quickly overpowered the man and pushed him off of Arianna. He threw a few jabs directly at the man's face and within seconds the man had ran away. Arianna watched in awe and was thankful that she had been rescued by the stranger.

"Are you okay," the man said, as he helped her get up from off of the ground. "I'm not sure. I don't know who that man was but I'm so thankful that you helped me. Thank you so much! I don't know what would have happened if you hadn't been around," she exclaimed. "No problem. I'm glad I could help but you have to be more careful out here. You shouldn't run out here this early alone because it's so many crazy people out here on these streets. The world is not as safe as it once was," he said. "You're so right. I usually carry mace and some other things on me, but I wasn't thinking clearly this morning," she said, as she stared at the handsome man who had just rescued her. "Well let me walk you back to your car," he asked. "Great. I'm not parked to far from here," Arianna said, as she smiled. She was happy that this stranger and mysterious man had been on the Drive. She had almost forget her manners as well and a very important question.

"Oh, I'm sorry. My name is Arianna, what's your name," she said. "That's a beautiful name. Are you married? You're so beautiful you must be with someone," he flirted. "No, I'm not with anyone but what's your name," she asked. "I'm sorry. My name is Kyle," he said as they approached her car. "Listen why don't you take my number in case you need me again. I'd love to help you out a bit more often. Preferably sooner than later," he said. "Sure, I can do that," she said, as she pulled her cell phone out of the car and put his number in her contacts. She also gave him her number and then she got into her car and began to drive away.

As she drove she thought about calling the cops and making a report. She had been assaulted and even though she had been saved by this handsome stranger, she wanted to make sure other women were not a risk. She called the cops and they asked her to head to the district to make a formal report.

Later That Evening

The first thing Face noticed when he walked into the house was his wife sitting on the sofa. Tasha was relaxing and sipping on a glass of sweet red wine. She had the lights dimmed and the soulful music of her favorite singer, Eric Benet, was grooving through the calm night air. Face smiled as he watched his wife sing along to the song with her eyes shut. She was in the groove but once she felt a gaze upon her, she quickly opened her eyes and was startled.

"Baby, how long have you been standing there," she said, as Face walked over to her and sat down beside her. "For just a few moments but long enough to know that man really has you in a good move. He got that feel-good music for you huh," Face played, causing his wife to laugh softly as he pulled her into his arms. "You know, he has a great voice. I likes me some Eric Benet, but I loves me some Face," she said, kissing her husband on the lips. "Good answer baby. Yeah, real good answer. I know your birthday is coming up soon. Maybe we could go to his concert," Face asked. "Really, I would love that," she said. "Good, well enough of Eric. I think your husband wants a piece of you now," he said, laying her down onto the sofa.

They exchanged a heated kiss before Tasha interrupted him. "Suri is at Veronica's and Norman is upstairs asleep. Maybe we should head upstairs just in case he comes down," she said. That is a good idea because once I get started with you I know those lungs are going to have one hell of a workout tonight," Face said.

"Oh really," Tasha said. "Yeah, you know what it is," he said, as he slapped his wife's ass as they walked towards their bedroom. "Where's mom at," he asked, as they entered their bedroom and he closed the door behind him. "She's sleep already. She had a personal training session today and he wore her out," she said. "Good. Now it's your turn. I hope you're ready for this workout because you're gonna need all your energy for this training camp. You might need an oxygen mask too," Face said, as Tasha laughed at him.

Tasha enjoyed the playful side of Face. He was often serious with the amount of business and problems that were always weighing him down. So tonight she was ready for the softer, lighter side he displayed but she also knew what he was about to lay down on her was going to be serious. Face was no slouch when it came to maintaining her kitty. He was all man in their bedroom and she succumbed to his every wish and demand, as he took charge and fulfilled her every sexual desire and need.

Doc had butchered up Father Jenkins' body as if it had been cattle. He had freezer bags full of the Father and spent a week making meals with his parts. Doc was a full-fledged cannibal. At the end of the week the only thing he had left of the Father was his bones; which he disposed of in the City's trash truck.

Marabella also feasted on the Father but Doc never told her that she was eating on human flesh. He finely chopped up the meat or sautéed it, so it looked like chicken or beef, and even liver. She was truly a slave to Doc and very miserable but she had no way to escape. She was monitored twenty-four hours of the day. Doc kept her chained up most of the day and he never allowed her to go outside. She was forced to have sex with her newly healed but often bruised vagina, and made to do housework as if she was a loving wife.

Inside this house of torcher there was no escape but there wasn't a day that went by that Marabella didn't think of how she would get away.

Marabella's life had forever changed. Whenever she gazed into a mirror she was always in disbelief. She didn't recognize herself. She was so far removed from her former self as a man that she couldn't remember what she used to look like. At times she thought she was stuck in a nightmare but inside she knew this life had become her reality. She had breast where their used to be pecks and a pussy where there was once a dick. It was a feeling that ate at her soul and often feasted upon her brain.

Marabella resented and hated Doc. She couldn't stand the sight of him but had to force herself to put those feelings away. She knew that she had to use her mind to out play him and if given the chance she would slit his throat the first chance she got. Doc was a sociopath. He was a cannibal, a killer, and a man obsessed with eating eyeballs.

At night Doc would read literature on torcher and serial killers. He studied this work and proclaimed himself a master killer and a leader in the field of torture. He never missed his favorite television series, C.S.I. He would yell at the screen whenever a criminal was caught for their crimes. He would shout out to them what they had done wrong and what they should have done to get away with the perfect crime. He was a lunatic and Marabella wanted him dead.

Marabella had only two options left. She had to escape and if that didn't work, she had to kill Doc and then free herself. She could not spend the rest of her days living as Marabella. She had tons of money that no one knew about. She knew that she may never be able to return to her former life as a man, but if she could get to her money she'd figure something else out.

City Line Avenue

Inside of the parking lot of the Friday's Restaurant, Kyle patiently waited inside of his Lexus. As the music of the Inner City Hustlers flowed from his speakers he couldn't help but think about the day's event. Arianna was a beautiful woman and far more stunning once he saw her up close and personal. Kyle sat there staring at her phone number on his cellphone. Moments later a man arrived and entered into the Lexus.

"Man, you happy now? You ain't have to beat me like no fuckin dog though man. Those wasn't no play hits like we practiced. You went too damn far," the man said. "I'm sorry man, I got caught up in the act," Kyle laughed, as he passed the man ten one hundred dollar bills. "Thanks Kenny. She really thought you were about to kill her ass," Kyle continued. "Yeah, we scared the hell out of her," Kenny said. "Right, but make sure you keep this between us. This can't get out ever," Kyle said in all seriousness. "No, I ain't saying a word," Kenny said, as he made the gesture as if he was zipping up his mouth.

When Kenny exited the car, Kyle watched as he drove off. Then he pulled out of the crowded parking lot and headed to North Philly to meet Quincy and Reese.

22nd & Norris Streets
North Philly

Inside a small brick row home Reese and Quincy sat at a large table that had lots of money on top of it.

Stacks of hundred, fifties, twenties and tens covered the table and the surrounding floor. Reese and Quincy kept watch as five workers counted and staked the money into large black duffle bags. Two armed men sat out front and kept watch for any possible distractions or problems. So far, the workers had over four million dollars counted and bagged up; with lots more money left to count.

"Where's Kyle," Reese said. "He's out taking care of that problem," Quincy replied. "Good. That bitch needs to be out of here. She thinks she can fuck with a boss and walk away without consequence. That bitch trippin," Reese said as he grabbed a bag and carried it towards the door. "Kyle's on her ass. He'll handle her," Quincy said, as he stood up and followed Reese to the door. "I love his loyalty," Reese said, as a smile came upon his face. "These days you can't buy that type of loyalty," Quincy said, as the two men carried a few of the bags to their van.

Chapter 16
Bala Cynwyd, PA

Face looked over at his mother and he was pleased to see her back to her old self again. Her near death experience was traumatic and devastating to him; and now it was good for him to see her back in high spirits. Face spared no cost when it came to providing his mother with the best physical therapy and he got his money's worth. She looked great and had told him that she never felt better; but the internal scars of the trauma would not be able to heal so quickly.

Pamela had an interior turmoil that ate away at her. She knew how to smile pretty so her family wouldn't worry but inside there was pain. She carried the weight of knowing at any moment someone could kill her son. She knew he was a target and even with his armed security and all the precautions he took, he would never be out of harm's way. Then with the unexpected and haste move into their new home, she knew that another incident must have occurred for them to uproot so quickly. Together, Face and Pamela had been through some coarse and uneasy times but the love she had for her son would carry her to hell and back to rescue him; or she'd die with him if she had to.

"Are you okay Face," Pamela asked as she sat beside her son on the couch. "Yes mom, I'm fine," he replied. "Boy, you're my son and I can always tell when something is on you heavy. What's up," she said, sensing that her son was dealing with something severe. "I'm good mom. I just have a lot on my mind right now," he said, not wanting to add any more pain on his newly recovered mother.

"Well remember what I told you…Never run from your fears. You have to face them all as they come. Life is like a big chess game and in this life you have proved that you're a king. You have to make sure you keep people around you that will help you stay in your position, and don't ever let your guard down," she said, as she looked at her son to see if she could read his mood and gain some insight to his troubles.

"I'm okay mom. My team is loyal mom," Face said to his mom with assurance. "Okay. Make sure the king doesn't show his crew any signs of weakness; and a true king will always respect another king. I raised you to be a leader, you decided to rise up and be a king. You're strong and I respect you. I want you to be sure in what you're doing and about the life you've chosen. Let your heart and soul guide you to all your victories and live like a king always. Because when you are gone from her, you will leave a lasting legacy," Pamela said, as she reached over and gave her son a warm, loving hug. "Thanks mom, I love you," he said, as he gave his mom a kiss on the check. "Love you too Face," Pamela said.

Tasha stood a few feet away from her husband and mother-in-law as she smiled happily at the close bond the two of them shared.

54th Street & Chester Avenue
Southwest Philly

Inside of the stolen car the eyes of the two masked men gazed upon four members of Face's drug organization as they carried black duffle bags into a house. The two men had been plotting on the house for a few weeks and were interested in getting their hands on what they knew was inside of those bags; cash or a large amount of drugs. On any given day twenty-five to a hundred kilos of cocaine made its way in and out of the house.

The two men sat silently for a moment as they realized what they had to do next. They grabbed their loaded 9mm and took a few deep breaths as they readied themselves to make a move. "You ready Bishop," Corey asked. "I'm ready, he replied.

The two men burst out of the car. They aimed their guns as they began to squeeze their triggers at the workers without delay. All four of the men were caught off guard and their attacker's bullets were hitting their targets dead on. Within two minutes the masked men had leveled the men to the ground, killing them with head and torso shots. The two men raced over to the bags and without checking the contents; they knew they had come up.

Four men dead and over two hundred kilos of pure cocaine stolen from Face's organization. This was a first for Face and the biggest hit he had ever taken.

"We did it," Corey said. "I told you it was sweet," Bishop said, as she drove the car down Woodland Avenue. "Fuck them niggaz. They shouldn't be getting all this money up southwest anyway…this our fuckin hood," the man continued. "Right, plus they work for Face and Reese and you know how I feel about them. Fuck em," Bishop said, as he pulled off his mask. "Corey, I just came home and I needed this come-up. If I ain't eatin then I'm killing anyone who stands in the way of me feeding my family and myself. I'm about to be the boss around here."

Both men were geeked up as Cory looked into one of the bags and saw the pure white. "We rich as shit," Corey said. "Not yet youngin. We still got to get rid of this shit," Bishop replied.

This score was going to be life changing and they knew they would now need to protect themselves because once word got out it was them they would surely have a price tag on their heads. They were fully aware of that before they robbed Face but the reward was worth the risk.

Raymond "Bishop" Lewis was a short and short tempered, dark-skinned man that was a known street thug from Southwest Philly. He had spent half of his twenty-nine years in and out of state prisons for robbery and selling drugs. He had murdered over ten men, mostly drug dealers, and with the four he had just added to his list, he could care less if he had to add more. People on the streets knew he would off you and never look back, and he would definitely kill you if he thought you would rat on him to the cops. He had no conscious and his only motivation was to get a quick score and to make his life easier. He wasn't about starting from the bottom; he wanted to get to the top as fast as possible. He ran a small crew of known thieves called "The Takers" and his younger cousin Corey was a part of his team. He trusted Corey with his life but Corey would be a fool to give him the same respect. Although Bishop wanted to help his cousin out there was no loyalty in him. Bishop wanted what he wanted, and would do whatever he had to do to get it; even if that meant double crossing family.

Bala Cynwyd, PA

Face heard his emergency phone vibrating and he reached to pick it up. "We just coded," Quincy said. "Face sat up from his bed. Tasha was knocked out beside him. "How many men," Face asked. "Four." Face took a deep breath and nodded his head. "How many cupcakes did the bakery lose," he asked. "Two hundred," Quincy said. "Okay, take care of the bakeries people. Spare no expense and make sure you get a crew in there to get things straight," Face said, as he started to think about what he had to do. "I'm on it. I'll see you in the morning," Quincy said as he hung up the phone.

Face lay back in his bed and closed his eyes. He would deal with the problem in the morning because right now he didn't want to disturb his wife. He knew this was a problem but his entire family was still dealing with the new move, and trying to get past the sins of Father Jenkins. He had his men on it and when the morning came he could go out into the field and tackle the situation head on.

Chapter 17
Washington, D.C.

Vice President Charles Bush sat patiently in the back of the black limousine as he waited for Paul Warner to arrive. Today was a special day but sad all in the same; it was his former friend and lover, C.W. Watson's birthday. Since Watson's tragic death there hadn't been a day that the Vice President didn't think about him. He had shared a bond with this man that was stronger than any woman he had met and it didn't sit well with him that a Kingpin in Philadelphia had something to do with Watson's demise.

The Vice President watched as Paul Warner pulled up in his black Chrysler. He quickly got out of his car and climbed into the limo.

"What's up with the new car," The VP asked, as they shook hands. "I didn't want to drive the government issued vehicle around Philly. People can spot an agent a mile away so I needed to blend in," Paul said. "Okay. Where did you get it from," The VP asked. "The car," Warner responded. "Yes, the car," The VP said. "It's a rental," he said. "Okay. That's smart. So what's going on in the city of brotherly love," The VP asked. "I'm still gathering intelligence on Face's organization. I have the I.R.S. doing an audit of his wife's real estate company, and the local F.B.I. director is pulling names, addresses and gathering informants that could help with this investigation," Paul Warner said. "Good, did you find anything yet that sticks out," The VP asked. "Nothing of real importance but Mike Conway was working for Face. I saw a receipt from their real estate company amongst their files. Also, I noticed that Mr. Conway was in D.C. when Peter Greenberg was kidnapped. He was surely working with Face, and that's why he'd dead now," Paul Warner exclaimed. "You're doing a great job. Keep at it and make the C.O.U.P. proud. You have to get that nigga and that bitch Veronica too," The VP said. "Sir, I won't let you down. As soon as I locate Face he's a dead man," Paul Warner said, as he shook The Vice President's hand. "Paul, I'll see you soon. I have a cabinet meeting with The President so I have to go. Get back to Philly and take care of this problem of ours," The VP said, as Paul shook his hand and exited the limo.

Four Days Later
Center City, Philadelphia

Veronica lay across her bed as she watched the Lifetime cable channel. Since the murder of the undercover C.O.U.P. agent Carter, she had been keeping a low profile and staying under the radar. She no longer partied at some of the elite social events and she stayed out of the public eyes as much as she could. Her life had changed since Carter's murder and her sex life took a hit too. Veronica's high sex drive had to find pleasure with her sex toys because she could not risk going back to her client files. She was a highly sought woman after but she couldn't take any chances. Her life was on the line and she was wanted by the government. She still had her tapes but even with that insurance she didn't feel safe.

Face made sure he made it clear to Veronica that the U.S. government was the biggest crooks on earth. He repeated, "Never get comfortable. They don't stop until they get what they want," to Veronica until it stuck. So most days Veronica's life was centered around Pamela and Tasha; as well as the kids-Suri and Lil Norman.

On the weekends she found pleasure in playing her role as godmother to Suri. Suri would come visit with Veronica and the two played dress up, did each other's hair, and put on makeup, as well as having their nails painted. Face called often to check on them when Suri visited. He trusted Veronica because she was family and he loved to see his girls happy, but he didn't trust his enemies.

After the Lifetime movie ended, Veronica showered and got dressed. She then got into her new BMW and headed towards Pamela's.

In the middle of the afternoon the sounds of heated, steamy, vigorous love making played throughout the bedroom. For a week straight the two young lovers were entangled in a world of blissful non-stop sex.

Arianna had found a knight in shining armor with her new man Kyle. Since the day they met and he had saved her, she had been smitten with him. He made her feel so comfortable that she let her guard down and shared her darkest secrets with him. Even though Kyle knew who she was, her connections, and her history, he played along and pretended to be surprised as he comforted her. He listened to Arianna as she told him how much she hated Face, and how she blamed him for killing off her family. She was so comfortable that she even told him that she had tried to kill Face, but she wasn't sure if she had succeeded.

Kyle was confused. A part of him wanted to kill her for shooting Face but another part of him wanted to continue to make love to her juicy, tight, sugary walls forever. They were both sleeping with the enemy but she had no idea Kyle was contracted to eliminate her and send her to the afterlife with the rest of her family.

"Kyle, you've changed me for the better. I haven't taken my pills since we've linked up. You really make me feel safe," Arianna said, as the two took a break from their love-making session. "Good, you don't need that shit anyway. That shit ain't no good for you," Kyle said, as he grabbed Arianna closer in his arms. "You're so right. I'm going to get rid of them," she said, resting her head on his chest. "I don't know what I would have done without you in my life. I'm really serious. You saved me on so many levels and I don't think I'll ever be able to repay you," Arianna continued, as she spoke freely allowing herself to be vulnerable to Kyle.

Kyle was quiet knowing he was connected to the man she hated most. Face was his boss and he had always been loyal and a dependable member of Face's crew. He didn't know if the situation between them would work out but he wanted to believe that everything would make itself right in time.

"Why don't you say much," Arianna asked. "I enjoy listening to you baby. You haven't had someone you could trust or talk to, and I want to be that person for you," Kyle said, as he rubbed her hair and kissed her shoulders. "Yes, I need that very much but it seems like you have a lot on your mind too. Sometimes it looks like you're lost in a daydream or something. What do you think about," she asked. "No, I'm good. My mind is clear," Kyle said. "Good. We should leave Philly and get married," Arianna said. "Are you serious," Kyle said, looking intently in her eyes. "Yes, why not? We don't have any family here and we love each other," she said. "What about Face," Kyle asked. "I'm over it. We can make a family and leave my past here. I'm over him and this entire city. I need to go find my happiness and you are a part of making me happy," Arianna said.

Kyle was shocked. He had given her the dick and wanted to enjoy her but she was a bit more open than he expected. Not to mention Face had never wronged him. Face made him a top member of his team and Kyle had more money than any young man could ask for.

Arianna rolled on top of Kyle and said, "I love you Kyle. I want to spend the rest of my life with you." Kyle didn't respond. He didn't know what to do. He didn't want her dead and he didn't want to betray Face. Kyle wrapped his arms tightly around her soft body as she began to mount his dick. As her juices flowed from her kitty, Kyle found himself lost in a world of bliss. Arianna was beautiful, smart, sexy, and the type of woman he had always wanted. He didn't know what he would do but for now he let her ride his dick; and he enjoyed every moment of it.

Chapter 18
F.B.I. Building
6th & Arch Streets

For the past six months a group of agents had been investigating the murders of F.B.I. agents Powaski and McDonald. There was a two-hundred-thousand dollar reward for any information leading to the capture of their killers, but to date they had no promising leads. They did suspect that Face and his organization were behind their deaths but they had no proof. However, they knew it was no coincidence that the two men assigned to investigate Face and his crew had been murdered. And they were looking at linking Philadelphia's homicide detective, Ron Perry's murder to the crew because he too had been investigating Face when he was killed.

F.B.I. director James Conner had a gut feeling that they were all connected but he needed his team to provide him with the hard facts that would put Face behind bars for life. The closer the team looked into the case they saw the dots connecting. Ron Perry, Agent Powaski and McDonald, C.W. Watson, and former drug dealer turned informant, Vernon "Truck" Wilson, had all been killed and were all connected to Face's federal trial. Even the death of the former Nicaraguan cocaine Kingpins, Jose and Rico Gomez, appeared to be linked back to Face.

James Conner was not a fan of coincides and he needed to get to the facts to expose Face for the meticulous, sharp killer and Kingpin that he was. Norman "Face" Smith Jr. was in a league of his own, especially after he took on the U.S. government and won; but this street legend would not put a stain on James Conner's impeccable record. He would get his man and if not today, he knew he'd get Face some time very soon.

69th Street & Ogontz Avenue

Face, Quincy, and Reese all exited a tinted grey Chevy Impala and walked towards a large row home. When they approached the porch, the door opened and a tall, handsome, slim brown skinned man invited them inside. After closing the door behind them, he gave each man a hug. The man's name was Darious "King" Smith. He was Face's first cousin and he was the only blood relative that had been recruited into Face's empire. For over three years, King had been secretly working for his older cousin. Face didn't trust too many people but King had proved to be reliable, truthful, and constant.

Before King had gained employment with Face's organization he was a college basketball star at the University of Kansas. In his junior season he suffered a serious knee injury that derailed any attempt at a professional basketball career. Prior he had been scouted by several NBA teams and he was projected to be a first round lottery pick. King owed much of his success to Face because his cousin had always been there for him. Since King was seven, Face had paid for him to attend every basketball camp in America. He paid for his travel, food, and for anyone else who accompanied him to the camps. Face wanted his cousin to make it pro and when he heard of his knee injury it devastated him.

"What's up cuz," Face said, as he walked into the dining room. "Staying focused and getting this money. Just like you taught me," King said, as he gave his cousin a pound. "Good. You'll be on top for a long time as long as you stay focused. The money will to come to you," Face, said as he sat down in a chair.

King walked to the coat closet and pulled out a large green army issued duffle bag. He carried it over to

Quincy and handed it to him. "We good," King said, as Quincy opened the bag and examined the contents. "Yeah, we straight for sure," Quincy said as he looked at the large sum of money in the bag.

Face was pleased with his cousin King. He didn't disappoint him and he was a man of his word. He had always had the money he owed the team and never made any excuses about the amount of hours he put in.

"You good Lil Cuz," Face asked as he stood up and got ready to leave. "Yeah, I'm good. Just working hard so one day I can carry the torch just like you," King said, as he gave Face another hug. "Alright y'all," King said to Reese and Quincy as the men walked out of the door. Before Face left out he looked back at King and said, "If you do stand in my shoes you better remember everything I taught you, but you have to be better than me. No point of being the next leader if you can't outshine your teacher. Than that means I haven't done my job." King smiled and took the message to heart as he watched the men get into their car and pull off.

While in the car, Face sparked up a conversation about his young cousin. "What do you think of King," Face asked Reese. "He's a real good youngin. Plays his part and keeps it one-hundred. Why do you ask," Reese said. "Just wondering. How about you Quincy," Face said, as he sat back in the passenger seat. "I like him a lot. That's your peoples and he looks up to you. He plays his part. He's your father's sister only son and he idolizes you," Quincy said. "Why you asking though," Reese said, as his curiosity began to rise. "Man, you know he's playing chess right now. Look at him with his thinking cap on," Quincy said, as the men started to laugh.

"I know you man," Reese said. "We have a lot more years left in this game so don't start thinking to prematurely. He's definitely a prospect but you ain't going nowhere anytime soon are you," Reese asked seriously. "No, I was just asking," Face said.

As they continued to drive, Reese kept looking at Face making sure he wasn't thinking about walking away from the game. They had a lot of years in and Reese knew Face had a lot left to make their crew the most notorious and wealthiest team on the east coast. He didn't want Face thinking about retiring just yet.

When the trio parked Face got out of the car and said his goodbyes, as he walked towards his Mercedes. He started up his car and pulled off down the street. He used his touchpad radio to place on Kem, whose soulful sounds not only relaxed him but helped him think. He thought about what Quincy had said and he knew he was right. Face had something on his mind. He was a chess player and needed to stay as many steps ahead of everyone as he could.

King walked upstairs and went into his bedroom. He sat down at his desk and turned on his computer. Every night he would Google the names of some of the biggest Kingpins and studied their moves. For hours he would be engrossed in their lives as he tried to learn from their mistakes, so he could avoid any of their downfalls. He knew in order to be the best he had to study the best. His cousin was a master at the game and King knew one day he wanted to sit on the throne. Being a leader was in his blood and if the time ever came for him to take over, he would not let his mentor Face down.

3rd & Chestnut Streets
Old City, Philadelphia

Sitting on the corner of 3rd street, Paul Warner sat inside of his car as he waited for Timothy Feeney to arrive. He had only been waiting for a few minutes before Timothy pulled up and parked his black ford Taurus. As he nervously got outside of his car, Timothy Feeney looked to make sure no one was following him. He rushed over to Paul Warner's vehicle and got inside of the car. He then passed Paul Warner an envelope, as sweat formed on his forehead.

"That's the entire report," Paul asked. "Yes, that's our full analysis on the T&F Real Estate Company. We did a thorough investigation and unfortunately…we didn't find anything wrong. They had a really good team of lawyers and accountants that provided us with everything we asked them for. They are clean and all their financial records indicate and support that fact," Timothy Feeney said nervously.

Paul sat silent. He was angry but didn't want to do or say anything before he could think about his next move.

"Do you know what their company approximate worth is," Paul asked. "Yes. The company's estimate worth is one-hundred-and twenty million and they are ranked highly out of the top U.S. real estate companies," Timothy said, as Paul nodded his head.

Paul was incensed but he didn't want to show agent Timothy. As the two talked about the report, neither noticed the yellow cab that had been following Mr. Feeney's car. In the back seat of the cab was private investigator Vince Harris. After Tasha told Face about her suspicions of I.R.S. Agent Timothy Feeney, Face quickly put a tail on him.

With his Cannon 5D camera, Vince snapped a few photos of the men before telling the cab driver to pull off down the street. He was determined to find out who was the mystery man Timothy Feeney was reporting too. His reputation was on the line as well as a five thousand dollar bonus.

Chapter 19
One Week Later

For an entire week Bishop and his cousin Corey had been able to rob three more of Face's drug houses. They killed five more workers on their vicious robbing spree. They had taken over one-hundred thousand in cash and two-hundred-and-sixty-eight Kilos of cocaine. Bishop and Corey had no fear of the legendary Kingpin because they were knocking down his houses like it was child's play. They had heard all the rumors about Face and Reese but they were writing their own ticket. They had one agenda and that was to be paid; which they had managed to do with ease.

Bishop and Corey sat around in the house on Baltimore Avenue. They counted the large sum of money they had taken in blood and gazed upon the pure white they had at their disposal.

"Sweet, sweet, sweet," Bishop said, stacking a pile of cash on the table. "Southwest Philly is mines," he continued. "Fuck Face and whoevers riding with him," Corey shouted. "Don't get carried away Corey. Somebody knows we are behind this so don't start acting stupid. Southwest is small and it's a bunch of bitch ass niggaz around here on Face's dick. We still gotta move this weight and keep our heads attached to our bodies while we do it," Bishop said.

"You're right. I was a little hype but I know the deal. I hate theses snitches out here and this new grade of niggas ain't worth shit. They tell so much they be telling on themselves and ain't nobody even ask them nothing. I fucks with the K.A.S. crew because they stay offing snitches. They take that *Kill All Snitches* lifestyle serious and I got mad respect for them too.

The two men had no idea that four men had already been paid for giving up tape on their location. Face had sent a crew of hit men to Southwest Philly. He was not about to let these two armatures put another hitch in his operations. They were about to learn a lesson about rumors and lies; anyone can make up a story and try to pass it off as truth but a rumor always has some truth in it.

West Philly

Doc had dosed off in his chair as he sat in his basement searching the Internet all night long. He was reading up on new torcher techniques and didn't realize how tired he was. Marabella stood by the back door as she plotted her escape. This was her one and only chance to get away from this sociopathic serial killer. She had had enough and death was starting to look like her only option if she couldn't get away from this monster.

As she looked back at Doc, who was deep into his sleep, she avoided all the traps and security alerts before slowly turning the doorknob and easing her way out of the door. She knew she would stick out like a sore thumb in the hood but the blonde haired woman made her escape. She began to run as fast as she could in her grey jogging suite-never looking back at Doc's house of torcher that had destroyed her life.

Bogotá, Columbia

Robert Fuentes had just gotten word from his U.S. sources that the United States government had indicted him on Federal and International drug charges. He was also wanted by Interpol and a few other foreign authorities. With over a billion dollars in assets, Roberto was prepared to put up a fight. He had already convinced himself that he would not be taken alive. He had seen his death in his dreams and knowing what the U.S. had done to the former Columbian Kingpins like Pablo Escobar and Griselda Blanco, he had already predicted their move.

Death before dishonor was his motto. “Let them come and get me,” Roberto said to his team of bodyguards. Carlos, his right hand man said, “Fuck the U.S., Fuck America, and fuck anybody who thinks they can come here and take what you’ve built.” Suddenly everyone in the room was yelling, “Fuck the U.S!” Roberto picked up his Ak-47 and he raised it high in the air and joined in on the chant.

“When they come we’ll give them the fight of their lives, “he shouted, as his men burst out in cheers.

Chapter 20
Center City, Philadelphia

Inside of the luxurious and large bedroom, Kyle laid back on the bed as he enjoyed the soothing pleasures from Arianna's soft lips. Pleasing her new man was all she wanted to do, all day and night long, and she wasn't alone. Every chance Kyle could get he would rush to be with Arianna. He had fallen hard for her and the more he was around he, the more confused he became. The lines were blurred and he didn't know what side of the fence he was on.

As his body began to show signs that his orgasm was at the head, Arianna began to slurp up and down on his dick faster and she moved her hand up and down his pipe to stimulate him as well. "AAHHHHHH," he shouted as his cum burst out and Arianna opened up her mouth to catch it all. "Yummy," she said, as she swallowed the warm, coating semen down her throat.

Kyle looked at her and the sight of her swallowing all of his cum, kept his dick rock hard and he was ready to plunge himself deep inside of her. "Lay down baby. Daddy needs some more of his kitty," he said, as he threw her down on to the bed. He thrust his hard dick into her super-soaked pussy and round three began.

Philadelphia Detective Roscoe Murphy was considered the best detective on the entire police force. He was placed in charge of the murder case of his former comrade, Detective Ron Perry. They had climbed the ranks together and now Roscoe was the head detective of a very busy homicide unit.

Roscoe Murphy stood at 6'4 and was light brown-skinned. He was a no nonsense type of guy with an immaculate employment record. He had been voted *Officer of the Year* twice by his peers and now he was working one of the biggest cases of his career. Finding the men who killed Ron Perry would be his honor and he knew the men who would break open this case were Face, Reese, Quincy, and Kyle. Each one was a suspect and they had the evidence needed to put the killing of Ron Perry to rest.

West Philly

"Doc calm down," Face said, trying to console his friend as Doc sat in his chair crying. A flow of tears ran down Doc's face as he yelled, "She's gone! She's gone!" Reese stood back trying his best not to laugh. It was one of the funniest sights he had ever seen because Doc was crying as if Marabella was his real wife; and even a real woman for that matter. Even Face had to try to conceal his laughter about the situation.

"I love her. Please help me get my wife back Face," Doc cried. "Doc, I got men looking all over the city for her. I can't have Peter running around this city," Face said. Doc became angry. He didn't like Marabella being referred to as Peter. In his mind and soul Peter was dead and had given new life to Marabella; the woman he was supposed to spend the rest of his life with.

"Marabella can't be out there. You have to bring her back to me. Please have your men find my wife. I need her home with me. She made a mistake but I'll forgive her as soon as she gets back," Doc cried out.

Reese couldn't help but laugh at Doc. He had never seen him this vulnerable before and it was too funny for him to hold in his laughter. Doc shot Reese a few angry glances and continued to talk to Face. Although Reese laughed, he knew they could not afford to have Marabella on the streets. She knew too much and posed a threat to them all.

"Doc I'm going to bring her back," Face said. Doc stood up from his chair and looked at his dear friend. "Face, promise me that you will. I need her back." Face put his hand on Doc's shoulder and said, "I said I'll bring her back and I will but you have to promise me you won't do anything crazy until I get her back. I need you to chill out Doc."

Doc agreed to behave and then Face and Reese walked to their car. Once they got inside both could no longer hold their laughter in. The car erupted as they cracked up about how Doc had performed. Neither had seen him cry and plead out as he did. They couldn't stop laughing as they drove off and helped with the search.

Chapter 21
52nd & Market
West Philly

Marabella was down on her knees giving a huge black man a blow job inside of a large brick row-home. She has surrounded by two other men as they waited in line for their turn. Prior to their sexual interactions, the three men were inside of a large truck when they noticed the lost blonde wondering the streets. They pulled over to offer their assistance and to their surprise the beautiful female had other thoughts in mind. She offered them each a sexual favor if they would provide her with three hundred dollars each. One at a time they had their turn with Marabella in the abandoned home. Even though initially Marabella felt disgusted she was in need of the cash, so she had no other choice but to make this money as quickly as she could.

Doc had made her life a daily nightmare and with the money she made she would run as far away as it could take her; until she could plot her next move. She didn't know who to trust or who would believe her outlandish story of how she was once a man named Peter, but she would never willingly go back to the man who had been brutally raping her-and passing it off as lovemaking; nor would she go back to eating his meals of flesh. She'd rather die than to rot in the house of torturer.

After Marabella had given up her body for sex and finished sucking the dick of the last man and spitting his cum on the cold floor, she wiped her mouth and stood up and fixed her clothes.

"Okay fellas, I need to get paid now," she said, staring at each one of them. "Here you are, it was well worth it," the huge black man said, as he passed all of their money to her. "Is there anything else we can do for you," he said, as the men walked towards the door. "Sure. If you can give me a ride to Florida or close to there that would be great," she said, flashing a quick smile. "Sorry pretty lady, I just can't do that. We're not headed that way," he said, as they walked out of the door.

Marabella followed them out and watched as the men got into their truck. They were smiling and felt fully satisfied at the unexpected sexual pleasures they had just enjoyed. As they began to pull off down the street, Marabella walked away. She knew Doc would be out searching for her and she needed to get out of Philadelphia as soon as possible. When she saw a cab approaching her she flagged it down.

The cabbie looked at the beautiful woman from his rearview mirror as she got into the back of his cab and he asked, "Where to?" He sensed that something was wrong with her because she had a nervousness way about her. He also wondered what a white woman was doing alone in West Philly; she surely seemed out of place. "Is there a Greyhound bus station around," Marabella asked, as she looked out of the window to see if anyone was following them. "It's not around here but there's one downtown. At ninth and Filbert," he said, as he continued to watch her in his rearview. "Okay, take me there please."

The cab driver pulled over for a moment. He didn't know this woman and wasn't sure if she was a drug addict, or something worst. He knew the streets of Philadelphia as well as the people, and if something didn't seem right he wasn't about to make a mistake that could cost him his life. He wanted to be sure he had a paying customer in his cab and not some lunatic who was looking for drugs.

"I need a deposit from you before we go any farther," he said. "No problem. I have money. I'll give you forty dollars now and if it's more, I'll pay once we get there," Marabella said as she passed the money to him.

The driver looked at the money because something was off about it. He had been given a lot of funny money in the past and didn't want to waste this trip downtown. As he held the money closer to his eyes he got the confirmation that he needed.

"Get the hell out of my cab. This money is fake," he yelled at her. "What? No way. I just got this money from someone. What do you mean fake," she questioned. "Listen chick, this shit ain't real. You got fake money and I ain't taking you nowhere. Get out," he demanded. "Please I would never give you fake money. Let me look at it," she asked. "You can look at it all day. The President on that bill is Will Smith," he screamed. "Oh my, I'm so sorry," Marabella said, as she looked at the money.

On the hundred dollar bill Biggie was on there and the fifty had a photo of Tupac. She was in such a rush to get the money from the men she had screwed, that she never unrolled it when they passed it to her. She had been tricked. Marabella had no one to blame but herself as she tore up the money and threw it to the ground as she exited the cab.

Chapter 22
Cherry Hill, NJ

Early the next morning Face was sitting on the sofa watching CNN on his large flat screen TV. He had already read through the Philadelphia Daily news and the Inquirer. Pamela walked out of the kitchen, sipping on a hot cup of black coffee. She took a seat next to her son and gave him a kiss on the cheek.

"Are you okay," his mother asked. "Yes mom. I'm fine," he said, as he muted the TV's sound. "I want to talk to you about something very serious," Pamela said. "What's that," Face said, now fully in tune to his mom. Pamela sat her cup of coffee down on the oak table and took a deep breath. She held Face's hands and looked her son straight in the eyes.

"I think it might be time for you to leave the game alone. You've more than made it. What you've accomplished is more than what you or I could have imagined," she said, as Face listened keenly to his mother as she continued on. "I think of how you escaped death, a kidnapping, and you beat one of the toughest opponents ever when you took on the government. You have wealth and power, and no one in your camp or your family wants for anything. You've made it son. If your father was alive he would be proud of you. I damn sure am. I just know in my heart that you can't continue on in this game for your entire life, unless you want to cut your time here short. This game makes very few exceptions and the rest of the people get claimed by the prison systems or the cemetery. I just want you to walk away from the constant worries. I don't want you looking over your shoulders no more. I want you to enjoy life…that's all I want for my son. I want you to grow old and enjoy life. I don't want to bury my son."

Face looked into his mom's eyes as teardrops began to fall onto her beautiful brown skin. He could feel the power of her words and their sincerity as she purged them from her soul.

"Mom, I love you. I have been thinking about leaving the game but right now I can't. When the time is right I'm going to make the right decision," Face said, as his mom became disappointed at his response. "Face, why can't you get out now? What's really stopping you," she asked. "Mom, if I leave now I still will be in harm's way. I have to deal with a few people before I can walk. My family's safety is always my number one priority. I am going to make sure you, Tasha and the kids are right. Trust me mom. I can't ask you not to worry but I have to ask that you trust me. I didn't get this far by being a fool. Just trust me mom."

Face wiped the tears from his mother's eyes as he hugged and comforted her. She knew her son and he said what he meant and meant what he said. He was a strong man but she knew he needed her support. She had to be there for him because he was a man in a tough position; a position that many lusted after but few had a clue of the weight placed on the seat holder's shoulders.

Pamela found the strength to tuck away her tears and continued speaking with her son. "Face, I'm here for you. Whatever happens you know that I'm here and nothing will ever change that. Just be safe and if you do change your mind tomorrow, I'll support that too," she said jokingly, as she picked up her coffee and began to watch TV with her son.

18th & Venango Streets
North Philly

Detective Roscoe Murphy was on a serious mission. He had reached out to every street informant that he knew had worked with Ron Perry before his tragic murder. On the corner of 18th Street, Detective Murphy parked his car and patiently waited inside. He watched as a few men stood around smoking on blunts and conversing, until his person of interest arrived.

A short, white man on a black motorcycle pulled up behind the detective and parked his bike. The man got off of his bike and made his way towards the car.

"What's up Detective, how are you," he said, as he sat in the passenger seat. "I'm doing okay. I'm working and trying to put some pieces together to help clear a matter up. How are you," Detective Murphy said. "I'm good. Just trying to stay alive on these streets. What did you want to talk about," Mack said. "Well, I need to know if Ron ever asked you to dig up any information on Face and his people," he asked. "Yes, that's all he ever asked me to do," Mack said. "So, what did you find," Detective Murphy asked anxiously. "I never found anything really. I know Ron wanted him convicted and was digging for info but I didn't have anything useful," the informant said. "Okay, if you find out anything make sure you call me. I need whatever you can find on Face."

Detective Murphy was very disappointed. Mack had been working as an informant for over six years for the F.B.I., The DEA, and the Philadelphia Police Department; but he had nothing to help Detective Murphy out. He had helped his employers put away some major players, but when it came to Face he had no insider information. For now he was useless to the detective and he was quickly excused from the car so he could go about his regular to-do activities.

As the detective pulled off he realized he was back where he started. He had nothing on Face and his department had no leads to assist him with solving this case. He would not give up though because tough cases were his high. He would turn over stones that had been turned over before until he got the answers he needed. He was thorough and knew that even if this case took longer than he wanted it to, it would be solved.

After Detective Murphy was gone from sight, one of the men who had been smoking on the corner reached into his pocket and pulled out his cellphone. He quickly dialed a number and waited for an answer.

"Yo wassup Skeet?"

"I just seen that snitch ass nigga Mack talking to the police again."

"Cool. Did you get that info for me?"

"Yes, I have it. When you want to take care of that?"

"As soon as possible. I can't stand a snitch!"

"Well I know where he be at all the time."

"Then you know what needs to be done."

"Yeah, I'm already on it," Skeet replied. After the call ended Skeet went back to smoking and talking with his friends.

West Philly

Doc was a nervous wreck. Since the day Marabella escaped he had cried each day and night. He felt lost without her and would walk the streets of West Philly searching for his self-appointed bride. However, the longer she was gone the angrier he became. "She's going to pay when she gets home," he said to himself as he walked to his refrigerator. He had one eyeball left and if she wasn't back soon he would have to kill someone to get him another pair of eyes. They were the only treat that could calm him during her absence.

Chapter 23
7:10 A.M.
Southwest, Philly

Inside of a house on 58th Street & Woodland Avenue, Bishop and his cousin Corey were knocked out on the living room sofa. There were empty Corona bottles everywhere and blunt roaches all over the coffee table. They had a small gathering at the house the prior night, and the special invited guest were a few females who had all joined them in the ecstasy fueled event. The two men lay on the couch completely hung over.

Across the street from the home was a van filled with four masked men who all wore the color of death. They had been waiting since last night for the perfect opportunity to strike, and the time had finally arrived. Not a soul was outside on the street as each man exited the van and cautiously approached the home.

As they moved onto the porch they watched and looked for the men. One of the men quickly looked into the porch window and saw both targets asleep on the sofa. Without delay, the door was kicked open and they quickly approached Bishop and Corey with their loaded guns aimed directly on them.

The men were so intoxicated that they didn't awaken. While one of the men searched the house for any stolen gun, drugs, and money, the others kept their aims on Bishop and Corey; who were both snoring loudly and unaware of how closely death was knocking on their doors.

Moments later the man came down the stairs carrying two green duffle bags, as he returned to the couch he pulled his gun back out. Quincy lifted up his mask and rushed over to Bishop and struck him in the head with his gun. The dazed man awake and nearly shitted himself at the image standing in front of him.

"Face wanted me to deliver a message to you," Quincy said. "What," Bishop said, trying to see if there was any possible way out of his situation. "He said to tell you to say no to drugs," Quincy said, as the four men began to light up the bodies of Bishop and the still sleeping Corey. In less than a minute the men's bodies looked like a polka-dot dress with an infinite number of holes on it.

The men rushed to get the duffle bags left upstairs and got into their van quickly. A few blocks away they turned into the ShopRite supermarket and pulled next to an Acura. Two men exited the van and began placing the duffle bags into the car's trunk. Within moments the car was headed to a fresh stash house in North Philly and the job they set out to do had been completed.

Downtown, Philadelphia

Inside the lavish Drake hotel, Paul Warner sat inside of his bedroom staring at his naked body through a large mirror. Years of wounds and scars covered his strong muscular body. As he stared at his missing left arm a bad taste grew in his mouth. He wouldn't rest until the people who had taken his arm had lost their lives. He knew all the culprits were connected to a single person, and that person was Face. The man at the top of his list had been the same man who was behind the savage murders of C.W. Watson and his wife.

"You can run but you won't hide from me Face," Paul said, as he stared in the mirror. He was now fixed on getting rid of Face. He had lost an arm and now Face had to lose his life.

Chapter 24
Early The Next Morning
Cherry Hill, NJ

Face sat back on the sofa reading the Daily News. On the front page the headline story read: *Double Homicide In Southwest Philly* and the article profiled the case.

Yesterday morning Philadelphia Police were called to the 5800 block of Woodland Avenue in Southwest Philadelphia as reports of gunshots were heard. Upon entering the home they discovered the body of two African American males, Corey Tillman and Raymond "Bishop" Lewis. Both men have heavy ties to the street and very lengthy criminal records.

In the city where crimes are heard but never seen, the Police have no witnesses and fear this crime will be added to the growing list of unsolved cold cases.

Face sat the paper down and nodded his head. He was pleased with the brief piece he had read and as long as they were dead he didn't need to read anymore. He was not about to let two fools disgrace his organization and get a pass. He was aware that in his line of work death was the only punishment he could give to his enemies; because to overlook them or give them a pass meant his life could be taken next. He was not about to slip up on the account of two nobodies.

Standing up from the sofa, Face walked down to the basement. He approached the large flat screen TV monitor hanging on the wall. The screen showed images of the grounds surrounding his home and the entire house. This security and camera system was the best money could buy and in addition to the two armed guards, he felt it was a needed necessity to keep his family safe.

However, he knew he had to do more. The only sure security was to get rid of the man hunting him.

Center City

"Please tell me what's wrong," Arianna said, looking over at Kyle as he stared at the wall. "Kyle…Kyle, do you hear me," she asked, as she reached out and touched him on the shoulder. "I'm fine, just got a lot on my mind," he said," realizing he had drifted off and was brought back to reality when she touched him. "You know you say that all the time. There is always a lot on your mind but that's not really saying anything," she said. "I know but I do," he repeated. "Is it about us," she asked, worried that they may have been having a problem she was unaware of.

Kyle looked her directly in the eyes and said, "I love you. I wish everything works out and my family can accept you like I have." She was puzzled. What family was he talking about? "Kyle, who are these people," she pried. "My family is my family, and leave it at that. Don't ask me about it anymore," he said, seriously. "Okay baby, I will leave it alone. Just don't be upset with me. I love you and you're all I got left in this world," she said, as a tear dropped from her eye.

"Don't cry Arianna," Kyle said. He pulled her closely into him and hugged her tightly, as he reassured her he wasn't going anywhere. Kyle knew he could never kill her. Besides his mother, she was the only women he had ever loved. He was in love with her and wanted to be with her. However, he knew if he didn't kill her he was violating a direct order from Face. His life would be in immediate danger and with the questions about Arianna's whereabouts mounting, he didn't have much time to figure out what he was going to do.

Chapter 25
Bogotá, Columbia

Roberto Fuentes detested the United States government. He viewed the government and their employees as the biggest crooks on the planet, who had been allowed to destroy the likes of men like him for far too long. He was one of the few people who did not fear the United States He had never been afraid of death and would not let anyone or any administration dictate how he lived his life.

As he sat back on his couch smoking a Cuban cigar, a big smile was plastered on his face. A day earlier he had shipped nine thousand five hundred pounds of cocaine to the Bahamas; which was headed to America. This shipment was the largest he had ever disrupted and it was headed to his loyal friend, Face.

Face was the only man that Roberto trusted with large amounts of cocaine. Not only did Face have the man power to move the product but he had locations that Roberto could discreetly ship them to. Roberto knew that his days were possibly numbered because his sources at the Columbian embassy told him that he was listed as the number-one most wanted man with the C.I.A. and the F.B.I. agencies. With Bin Laden gone, the focus was now placed on him and the violent Los Rastrojos Cartel.

As the smoke from his cigar drifted in the air he thought about his demise. He knew he would not run like a coward and he dreamed about dying in a blaze of gunfire. He was prepared for a fight because he would never allow himself to be captured and have his pictured plastered on photos across the U.S. law enforcement agencies.

West Philly

Marabella needed a way out of Philadelphia and it was proving to be a lot harder than she had thought. She was afraid to go to the police because she was embarrassed about her situation and didn't want anyone to know she had been a man. Doc was on the streets searching for her and she was well aware of that fact. She knew he would never rest until he had her back in his clutches, so she was very hesitant when someone spoke to her; and even more fearful when people looked at her as she walked through the streets of West Philly.

It had been two days and the only place she found to rest was in an abandoned building. She was dirty and her body had a stench. She needed a bath but her current living quarters did not provide for a tub or running water. She was currently living in squalor and unable to think of a plan to remove her from these vile conditions. As she sat on the floor contemplating a way out, she had no idea the abandoned property she was in was only a few blocks from where Doc lived. Face's men had passed this house a few times during their search and it had been pure luck that she hadn't been spotted yet.

Germantown Philadelphia

Paul Warner didn't have many friends and he wanted to keep it that way. The only people he trusted were the members of the top secret organization he belonged to, The C.O.U.P.; everyone else he viewed as a potential enemy. So as he worked on this case alone, he felt comfortable and eager to add another trophy to his collection so he could return to the C.O.U.P and share his success of killing Face with his friends.

For a week Paul had been driving his black Chrysler 300 around the streets of Philadelphia. In order to learn the city he knew he had to be a part of it. He saw the underlying issues of poverty and witnessed the violence firsthand. Each day he would hear of shootings, homicides, rapes, kidnappings and robberies as the news was broadcasted on the local radio stations. He listened to learn about the city but he had no concern for the victims or the offenders. He actually got enjoyment out of hearing the black-on-black crimes because he had a deep hatred for African Americans, Hispanics, and Jewish people. He viewed them as nothing more than scum who wasted space on earth. He had been a fan of Hitler and often thought of how great the world would have been if the crazed dictator would have completed his original plan.

Paul and his hatred often brought conflict to his front door. He hated that the country had a black president and he wanted nothing more than to kill him and have him replaced with a Caucasian leader. He had talked about killing the president to members of the C.O.U.P. but they advised against such a plot. They knew the heat would be too grand, even for their powerful organization, but Paul still wanted to eliminate him. The thought of a black man running the country sickened his stomach and he wanted the man out, even if he had to carry him out himself.

As he continued to drive around the city, taking mental notes and observing, he never noticed that someone was watching his every move. Vince Harris was on his heels. Paul Warner had murdered his associate, Mike Conway, and Vince was determined to settle the score. Vince had done his homework on Paul and knew about his connections to the C.O.U.P. but that wouldn't stop him for going after him. Paul would make a mistake and he would slip up; but for now Vince did his secret surveillance like Face had asked him to.

Chapter 26
Sunday Morning
Southwest Philadelphia

Inside of the United Methodist Church, the small sanctuary was packed and police informant Mack Wooden, along with his wife and child, were seated in the middle aisle. They read along in their bibles as the pastor gave his sermon.

For over five years Mack had been a paid employee for the Philadelphia Police Department as well as the local F.B.I. offices. The information he provided had convicted four of the city's top drug dealers and he testified at each of their trials; and he was a regular participant at the Grand Jury hearings. When Mack wasn't riding around with his Ghost Rider motorcycle gang and gathering critical information for the authorities, he was a devoted husband and father. He had been married for three years and his son, Mack Jr., was the apple of his eye.

As Mack sat there reading the book of John, he and no one else noticed the two men who had calmly walked through the church doors. No one paid them any attention as they scanned the crowd. When they caught sight of Mack, who had his head down as he read the bible, they walked towards him.

Upon approach, they reached into their jacket pockets and pulled out their firearms. One man had a .45 and the other had a .357 magnum. Soon as their target was in arm's reach, the men turned to Mack.

POW!!! BOOM!!! BOOM!!!

They unloaded their bullets into Mack's chest and head and they didn't hold back. He stood no chance as his wife and son screamed and ran away from their dying love. The church-goes ran for cover as the chaotic scene unfolded. No one could have imagined that a church would be at the center of a murder crime scene, as they tried to escape the church for safety. The two men quickly made their exit to a waiting car outside of the church. The getaway driver was geared to go as he rushed off, quickly driving the killers of Mack Wooden away as his corpse bled out on the church pew.

Moments later the car pulled into a garage near the Tasker Homes Housing Projects. Quincy and Kyle were inside of the garage waiting for the men's arrival.

"It's done Q," Skeet said, getting out of the car. "I made sure that snitch took a bullet to the center of his dome," Skeet said. "Good shit," Quincy said, passing Skeet his fees for carrying out the hit. "It's all there and I threw in something extra. I'll call you soon and thanks for the info," Quincy said, as he and Kyle climbed into their grey Range Rover and drove off.

Skeet and the two other men involved in the hit began to gather their clothes, guns, and gloves as they began to get rid of the evidence; including the car. They had made a quick ten thousand dollars each and knew that as long as they stayed on Face's team they would have plenty more money coming their way.

Skeet, who was a low-ranking member in Face's organization, had been on his team for over three years. It was his job to keep his ears to the streets and find out as much as he could about anybody who posed a threat to Face; as well as recognizing the snitches who worked for the authorities. Once he identified a snitch, he called their names into Quincy or Kyle, and then he gathered up information on who they worked for, as well as where they lived, who they hung around, what type of car they drove; and the easiest way to eliminate them. Skeet was a very important link to Face's empire and the team made sure he was compensated well and made to feel like a part of the family.

As Quincy and Kyle drove in the Range Rover down Broad Street, Quincy noticed Kyle wasn't himself. "Kyle, what's up," he asked. "Nothing. I'm good. "Oh, cause you've been distant lately," Quincy said. "No, I've just been going through some personal issues but I'm good," Kyle said. "Personal issues? Nigga you sittin on millions and you've got everything anyone could wish for, so what personal issues you got," Quincy asked. "Money can't solve everything man," Kyle said, sadly. "Man what's up? You need to talk," Quincy said, as he stared at his friend and waited for his response. "Yeah, pull over," Kyle said, as Quincy found a place to stop.

After a long sigh Kyle sat back in his chair and confessed what had been going on with Arianna, and why he hadn't killed her.

Chapter 27
Amtrak Station
Monday Afternoon

The Amtrak train station was located in West Philly, at 30th & Market Streets. Inside of the large building thousands of commuters boarded and exited trains that traveled up and down the east coast. Face had gotten an emergency phone call and needed to be at the station. He had two of his most trusted men posted up by the main entrance as he scanned the crowded station.

After a few moments of searching, he finally spotted the person he was looking for. When he saw Gloria he quickly realized that she was not alone. As she approached him with the unidentified visitor, Face could not help but keep his eyes affixed to the stranger. Once they had reached him, Gloria gave Face a hug, while Face kept his eyes on the young man who was with her. A very strange feeling came over Face as he studied the features of the young man. It was like he was staring into the face of a younger version of himself. In that moment he knew that Gloria had kept a secret from him and that secret was now staring him in the face.

"Give me a second honey," Gloria said to her son, as he walked over to one of the benches and sat down. "So you waited fourteen years to tell me that you had my son," Face said, as the bass rose in his voice. "I'm sorry Face, I was scared. I didn't know how to tell you," she said, trying to plead her case. "You should have just told me. I'm not one of those dudes that don't look out for their children. I claim and provide for mine," Face said.

Gloria began to cry as the guilt she carried began to boil over. She had no right to keep this secret and should have told Face a long time ago. Her son watched as his mother cried and rushed to be by her side.

"Mom, don't cry," he said, hugging his mother. "No, I'm fine Samaj. This is Norman," she said, as he looked over at the man who shared his face. "He's my father," Samaj asked, as Face stared at him. "Yes, this is your dad," she said, as she placed her loving arms around her son.

Face was silent. He didn't know what to say to the young boy. All he could do was stare at Samaj who looked identical to him. Apart from feeling deceived, he felt delighted in being this boy's father.

"I wanted him to meet you Face, even if it's only once. Samaj is so much like you and he deserves to know the truth. I feel horrible but I can't change the mistake I've made," Gloria said, as more tears fell from her eyes. "I'm just glad you finally brought me my son," Face said, as he continued to gaze upon the young man's face.

For the next few hours, the trio sat down on the bench and talked. Gloria told Face how smart Samaj was and how similar the two behaved. She also shared with him about his athleticism because he was the point guard on his school's basketball team. In just a short span of time, Gloria had tried to catch Face up with the last fourteen years of their son's life; which she knew was impossible but she still wanted to give up as much information about their son that she could.

"So why did you wait to tell me Gloria? Do you need money," he asked. "No. I don't need for anything. I've made my own way and you should know that. I just didn't want to lie to myself and Samaj forever. My husband knows he's not Samaj's dad," she said. "What? He knows," Face asked. "Yes, he knows. I had a long talk with him and he's the one who said I needed to get in touch with you."

Face nodded his head. He knew that unless Gloria's husband looked just like him, there was no way that he'd be able to think Samaj was his son. There was no resemblance. Even Gloria didn't pass off too many of her genes because the young boy was a splitting image of his biological father. Face didn't need a DNA test to prove this was his son and his focus was now on the young man who had been staring and studying him while they talked.

"So where do we go from here," Face asked. "Like I said, I just wanted you two to meet. I'm not sure what's next or even if you wanted things to go past today," Gloria said. "Well, I'm going to see him again. If he wants that," Face said, as he looked to Samaj for an answer. The young boy looked at his newly introduced father and eagerly said, "Yes, I'd like to see you again."

Before they said their goodbyes and got on the train headed back to New York, Face asked Gloria to take a picture of Samaj and himself so he could have a photo in his phone. Gloria happily obliged his request and she was happy to see that Face was not denying their son. Under the circumstances everyone was doing well with their first visit.

After the train pulled away, Face stood and watched as his son made his way back to New York. He still didn't fully believe that he was a father to a teenager. He had pain in his heart because he loved his children and always wanted to be a responsible father. He didn't respect a deadbeat dad and he knew he had to find a way to get better acquainted with his son.

As he sat in the back of his Bentley, Face stared at the photo in his phone. There was a young man who shared his face, who had his blood; whom he had never known. This was a game changer for sure.

Chapter 28
23rd & Ridge Avenue
North Philly

Detective Roscoe Murphy couldn't believe what he was reading. This was not the news he wanted to see. His informant Mack had been gunned down in the middle of a crowded church and the killers had gotten away scot-free.

"Dammit," he yelled, as he tossed the Daily News on the empty seat next to him. "Who the fuck does this guy think he is," Roscoe screamed. He was frustrated and sped his car down the street as he thought about Face's criminal reach. His face was red as an apple and his heart was beating quickly. The disdain he felt for Face had now turned into hatred. He wanted Face dead and the impact of this crime had made him swear to take Face down at all cost.

Georgetown
Washington, D.C.

The members of the C.O.U.P. sat down at the large oval table. They were inside of a secret location in the elegant section of the city; where some of the members had lived. They were all waiting for the meeting to begin.

"I just got word from our friend Paul Warner that our problems in Columbia and Philadelphia will be taken care of very soon," Vice President Charles Bush said, as he stood up and addressed the party. The men and women all nodded their heads at the update. "Hopefully before the year ends," the executive of the C.I.A. said. "It will be. I was told it should happen within the next few weeks," The VP said. "Great news. Those worthless scumbags are hurting our country," a congress woman said.

Everyone at the table stood and joined hands, as they closed their eyes and waited for The VP to speak. "We are the power of this great country, this great land. We are the masters of the masters, the kings of the kings. We are the Gods and there is no one on this earth or in the universe higher or more powerful than us. We control life and we determine death. We are the All- Seeing Eye, the Alfa and Omega. What we say is law!"

At the close of his speech, everyone opened up their eyes and started to continuously shout, "C.O.U.P., C.O.U.P., C.O.U.P.!"

Cottman Avenue
Northeast Philly

Private investigator Vince Harris sat inside of his car and watched as the I.R.S. Agent Timothy Feeney walked out of his front door and got into his car. For over a week he had been watching the agent's every move because Face wanted to know everything he could about him. So far Vince found out that he was a senior executive at the local I.R.S. branch and he had been employed with the government for over twelve years. He graduated first in his class from Drexel University, with a master's degree in accounting and had no wife or children.

After getting into his car, Agent Timothy drove off. With his departure, Vince got out of his car and headed towards the agent's front door. Dressed in a Philadelphia Gas Work's employee uniform, he knocked on the front door twice before heading around to the back of the house. He knew from earlier surveillance that the agent kept the back window of his home open but he wanted to make the visit look official if anyone had been looking from the front door's view.

Vince quickly climbed into the back window and walked upstairs into the master bedroom. He saw a desk in the corner with a bunch of paperwork on top of it. He noticed several large envelopes but what drew his attention was one that had the words: *Sensitive Information: C.O.U.P*. written on it. Using his rubber gloved hands he opened the envelope. He quickly breezed through the papers and took pictures of each one with his iPhone.

Timothy Feeney was a paid employee of the secret society, the C.O.U.P., and this information was promising and very important for Face. Vince knew he hit the mother-load as the uncovered the names of other members of the society. The paperwork showed years of C.O.U.P. and I.R.S. corruption and Vince had proof of it all.

After he had gathered up all the information he needed, Vince left the home the same way he had entered it. He got back into his car unnoticed and realized how foolish Timothy Feeney was. Why would the man leave important documentation, such as the names and corruptions practices of the I.R.S. and the C.O.U.P. on a table for anyone to stumble upon; and why didn't he have a security system. What a fool, Vince thought, as he started his car up and pulled off.

Chapter 29
Center City

Veronica loved her god-daughter Suri as if she was her own child. Every weekend Tasha would let Veronica take Suri with her to her downtown condo. The pair went out to eat, shopping, and they also did some sightseeing-as they enjoyed the loving sights that center city had to offer. Veronica spoiled Suri with the newest fashions and the any toys that the young child craved. Since Veronica was childless and unable to have children due to a hysterectomy, this five year old had touched a part of Veronica's life that she would never be able to experience on her own.

Face and Tasha knew the joy that Suri brought to Veronica so they did not deny her the right to spend time with their daughter. However, Face was not going to send his daughter anywhere without security; so each time his daughter visited she was escorted with an armed guard-who stayed close by in case of any emergencies.

Today, Veronica and Suri took a trip to Macy's. The young beauty looked up to her auntie Veronica and said, "I love you mom-mom!" She was excited about the new pair of shoes that her loving god-mom had just purchased and when Veronica heard her goddaughter tell her she loved her, it always melted her heart.

Miami, FL

Frank "Underworld" Simms and his partner Craig sat down on the sofa inside of the luxurious suite at the Ritz Carlton hotel. Their new drug connect, Juan Sanchez and one of his men entered the room. They all shook hands and greeted each other like brothers would do. This was their third meeting so far and everything had gone well.

"Now I see you come highly recommended by our good friend, Face," Juan said. "Face has a lot of respect for you Underworld," he continued. "I have the same respect for him. He's loyal and I got love for men like that," Underworld said. "Do you know that Face sent you to me so you could avoid the mess he's got going on around him," Juan asked. "Yes, I'm aware of that. I heard there's a secret society out D.C. that's trying to come at him," Underworld said. "Yes that's an unfortunate truth. Face didn't want them to find out who you were, if they didn't already know of you," Juan said. "Yeah, like I said I have nothing but respect and love for Face. He has my back when many others would be worried about their own ass."

Juan looked at Underworld and said, "You remember what this man did. He saved you from a lot of shit that you might not have had the resources to step out of. The men who are after him have killed many and even gotten some of my Columbian bothers. They want my cousin Roberto and your brother Face erased. You are here to stay off of the radar because as far as we know, neither one of our names are on their list of targets. I'm running things for my cousin from here until we deal with these fuckers in that society. I need to be clear with you on one thing. Loyalty, respect, and honor are what I'm all about. I'll die by it first before I go against my honor. I know if he showed it to you, then you're the right man for me to be doing business with." Underworld looked at Juan and said," Face is a legend in the streets. Everyone knows he's no rat or a snake, and my legacy will be the same. I am who I've always been. I'm straight up and ain't nothing and no one ever going to change that."

Two Days Later

Inside of a secret stash house located in North Philly, Face, Reese, Quincy, and Kyle stood around talking.

"What the fuck you mean you love that bitch! That's the bitch who tried to kill Face man," Reese vented. "Calm down Reese," Face said, as he pulled Reese back from out of Kyle's Face. "Calm down? How can I calm the fuck down when this nigga talking about he fuckin love Hood's daughter. That bitch would have murdered you! I can't accept that," Reese continued.

Face tried to weigh his options. He loved Kyle like a little brother but he had placed him in a very awkward position. He had to make a decision. Kyle had been one of his top men and his most loyal; and he was one of a handful of men that he trusted with his life.

Quincy and Kyle stood side by side while Reese angrily paced the room. Reese was furious and wasn't trying to hear anyone out. In his eyes Kyle had violated Face by not killing the woman who had tried to kill their boss. Then he had the nerve to come at them with a story of how he had fell in love with the girl. Reese was pissed and he didn't understand why Face was deliberating. He felt the decision was clear and someone should have killed Kyle as soon as he walked in the door; but what Reese didn't know was the Face and Kyle had formed a solid bond while Reese was in prison. This decision Face was forced to make was not an easy one.

Face walked over to the window for a few moments and stood there in deep thought. He never liked to make a hasty decision if he could take some time and put some thought behind it. Suddenly, he turned around and walked over to Kyle.

"I made up my mind." Quincy, Reese, and Kyle all stood there in silence as they waited to hear the final fate of Kyle. "I'm not going to kill her or you but you have to leave. Get everything y'all got and leave Philly. You got two weeks and if I ever see you or her again, I won't hesitate to do the job you couldn't finish," Face said. "Are you serious man," Reese shouted. "That bitch tried to kill you! Her entire family has done nothing but cause you harm. How could you spare that bitch's life," Reese fumed. "Reese will you calm the fuck down! Kyle is going to take her and get out of Philly. I'm not killing the woman he loves. Yes he violated my order but I learned a long time ago that love will make you do some strange things; even the strongest of us tasted the poison in the war of love."

Quincy and Kyle stood speechless. Both men were satisfied with Face's decision, and even though Kyle didn't want to leave his city; he didn't want to end up in a body bag either. This was a good day for him and his new fiancé, Arianna.

"I don't believe this shit! That's a weak move man! What the fuck is happening to you," Reese shouted. Face walked over to Reese and with the most serious expression he had ever shown his friend he said, "Nigga I grew up and became wiser! Maybe you need to do the same and learn that death is not the answer for everyone." Reese snapped back, "Not even for your enemy!" Face said, "My answer was final. He's leaving town."

Reese was beyond angry. Face was everything to him and he felt Face had made a foolish move. He didn't trust Kyle after he broke their bond of loyalty and he wanted Face to change his mind, but he knew him well enough to know he had come to a final conclusion. Reese couldn't stand to be in the same room as Kyle so he rushed out of the house, slamming the door behind him.

"Thanks Face. I swear I never wanted to be in this situation. I didn't want to keep lying to you, and Quincy told me I needed to be straight up with you. I swear I'm sorry. I've been stressing over this day and night and…I'm just sorry," Kyle pleaded. "Two weeks. You got two weeks Kyle," Face said. Quincy looked over at this friend Kyle and said, "I wish you the best Lil Homey. Now get your ass up out of here before minds get changed," he continued, as Kyle rushed out of the door.

Chapter 30
60th Street & Lansdowne Avenue
West Philly

Driving down Lansdowne Avenue, two of face men spotted Marabella as she walked down the street. The car quietly pulled over and one of the men jumped out and pointed a loaded .40 caliber at her head. "Get the fuck in the car bitch," he ordered. Marabella didn't know who the two men were but she was sure they weren't police, and that they had ties to her capturer.

Twenty minutes later the hungry and filthy Marabella, screeched with fear when the men pulled in front of Doc's house. She tried to jump out of the car but the child lock feature on the vehicle had been activated. She till tried to escape the car as she began to punch at the glass window, until the passenger struck her in the head with his gun. "Clam down bitch before I fuck you up for real," he said. The driver of the car had already notified Face and Doc that they had apprehended Marabella and were waiting for Doc to come to the door.

Upon seeing his angered face in the doorway, the men took Marabella from the car and led her towards Doc. He hadn't been able to get a good night's rest since his wife escaped and it had been over a week that he had been able to enjoy his sexual pleasures with her as well.

As they got closer Doc squeezed the long syringed in his right hand that was filled with a clear substance. Marabella saw that he had something in his hand and she tried to get away again but the men quickly overpowered her, and lead her towards the Doc.

As soon as the men got Marabella inside of the house, Doc quickly slammed the door behind them. "You've really disappointed me Marabella. Now you have to pay," he said, as he plunged the syringe into her neck. The dosage was so powerful that in seconds she fell to the floor unconscious. "I have it from here fellas," Doc said, as he walked the men towards the door.

Once they were gone Doc gripped up Marabella and took her down into the.

Two Days Later
Cherry Hill, NJ

While Tasha paced the bedroom in tears, Face sat down on the edge of the bed. He held his head down as he stared at the floor. He had to tell his wife about his fourteen year old son Samaj, and that his mother was Gloria. The pain that Tasha felt was indescribable. She felt betrayed and her once happy home was now nothing more than a house of anguish that Face had created. He had been her everything and she never expected for him to have children outside of her. In all the years they had shared together today had been the worst day she had experienced with her husband.

"Face, how could you," she cried. Face stood up and walked over to Tasha and tried to console her. She pulled away from him and didn't want to be touched. His hands felt like knives that cut deep into her skin and she didn't trust or respect her husband at this time. "I never knew about the boy. Gloria just told me about him and I couldn't keep this to myself. What was I supposed to do? I had to tell you," he pled.

Tasha looked at her husband and she knew when he spoke the truth. She believed him but it didn't ease her pains. The man she loved had a child by another woman and there was no amount of words that could heal her current anguish.

"Why did she wait until now? Why didn't she tell you before," Tasha cried, as Face rushed to his wife and forced her into his arms. "I don't know Tasha. I swear I don't know. I'd never hurt you and keep nothing like this from you," he said. "But this hurts so bad…I swear this is eating at me," she cried. "Baby, I didn't know," he said. "How do you even know if it's your son? How can you be sure," she urged. "I saw him. I know he's my son," Face said. "So now they do DNA look-a-like tests. Let me see him then," Tasha asked. "No. I don't think you want to see him," Face said. "Yes I do. Show me. Where's the photo," Tasha demanded.

Face pulled out his phone. He showed his wife the picture of his son; whose spitting image dug a knife deeper into her heart. Just at the sight of the photo she knew the boy was his. She broke down and began to cry uncontrollably. Face bled knowing he had hurt his queen and soul mate. He loved Tasha and her happiness meant the world to him. As he held her, he could feel the pain as it poured from her body and all he could do was hold her in his arms as she purged it.

Pamela stood outside of their bedroom and had overheard the entire conversation. She was delighted to have another grandchild but as a woman her hurt ached for Tasha. She knew that there were times that words could not heal, and only time, and prayer would bring her away from the pain her soul was enduring.

Chapter 31
Center City

Inside their condominium, Arianna and Kyle sat in the living room talking. "Why are you in such a rush to move," she asked her man. "Because I told you it's time for us to go. You need to trust me on this," Kyle said. "I hear what you're saying but I got to school here. I would have to talk to them first and see if I could transfer to another place. There are also other lose ends I would have to tie up before I could move," she said. "But don't worry I will make sure I get it all done in two weeks. I love you and if we have to move than that's what we're going to do," she said as she kissed Kyle passionately.

"Hold on," Arianna said, as she rushed into the bathroom. Moments later she returned holding her hands behind the back. She had a wide smile splashed on her face. "Why are you cheesing," Kyle asked. "Because we're happy," she said. "We're happy? What are you talking about," Kyle asked.

Arianna brought her hands forward and showed Kyle the pregnancy test that was in her hands. She passed the test to him and said, "See, we're happy. You're going to be a father and we're starting our family," she said.

Kyle held the pregnancy test in his hands and he couldn't believe his eyes. The test was clearly positive as both lines showed up brightly. "How far are you," he asked. "Baby we're just a few weeks. Are you okay with this? Are you happy," she asked him. "Yes, I'm very happy," Kyle said, as a tear began to fall from his eyes. "This is the best news I've heard in a long time," he said. "Good, because I want to give you this child. You mean everything to me and sharing our first child together will only make us stronger and hopefully keep us bonded forever. Kyle sat back down on the couch with Arianna as tears continued to fall from his eyes. He was excited beyond words and speechless. It was just a few days ago that his life could have been ended, but he had been spared and now he had the chance to enjoy parenthood; and to live his life with the woman he loved. "Arianna I love you baby and from this moment on we are in this together. Me, you, and our child."

West Philadelphia

Doc stood a few feet away from Marabella's unconscious body. She lay naked and strapped down to a large operating table. For two days Doc had been having sex with her, all while he continued to keep her medicated and unresponsive. In addition to having his way with her, he also had been doing some operating on her. He implanted a small micro-chip tracking device into the back of her neck. The devise would keep a position on her for twenty-four hours, and the device was connected to Doc's smart watch. With just a touch of a button, he would locate her. This time Doc wasn't taking any chances.

As he stared at his beautiful wife, his lust grew for her. There was no one sexier than his creation and he could never let her get away from him again. She was his, his wife, and his life.

Bogotá, Columbia

The dark sky was filled with bright, shining stars and the moon was full. Roberto Fuentes was inside of his bedroom sleeping peacefully while his large private villa was surrounded by armed guards. As the guards patrolled the grounds, none of them noticed the swarm of camouflaged Navy seals that began to surround the property. Each man was equipped with a pair of infrared binocular frames and an M-16 rifle. The fourteen member seal unit was one of the best covert units in the world. They were the same team of men that had captured and killed some of America's most wanted and sought after fugitives.

With the cover of darkness on their side, the seal unit began to attack with precision. Their strategic plan allowed them to kill Roberto's entire squad of bodyguards. In less than three minutes they were out of the way and the commotion had awakened Roberto, who was still inside of his bedroom. As he looked up at his security camera he saw the Navy Seal until approaching his bedroom. He knew this day was coming and he was well prepared.

Roberto reached inside of his pillowcase and pulled out a small remote control device and a loaded 9mm pistol. He had made a promise to himself that he would never be captured and let the U.S. do to him what they had done to his godfather and mentor, Pablo Escobar. He would not be gunned down like a savage.

Three seals approached the bedroom door and with a click of a button, a loud explosion erupted as it blew up a section of his upstairs-killing the three seals instantly. The blast was strong and unforgiving; and it created a fire that began to burn the house. Roberto placed his gun inside of his mouth. This was his time to make good on his promise. It may not have been the exact replica of his dream but it was going to be his end. As he pointed the gun upwards towards his brain, he pulled the trigger and sent a slug straight out of the back of his head. He was dead.

The rest of the Navy Seal unit cautiously made their way towards the bedroom. They retrieved the bodies of their fallen comrades but one man had other plans as he opened the door to the bedroom. Upon entering he spotted the body of Roberto Fuentes on the bed. He continued to approach. Paul Warner had a look of hatred upon his face as he looked at Roberto. He was angry because he felt as if he had been cheated out of his kill. He aimed his gun and began to fire several slugs into the corpse of Roberto Fuentes.

When he finished placing several holes into the dead man's body, he took out his camera and photographed his latest victim to show the C.O.U.P. members. The fire began to rage and members of the Seal team called to him to get out of the house but Paul Warner had no fear of the flames. He stood over the body and enjoyed the sight of its holey exterior.

In less than two hours Paul Warner would be on a private jet headed back to Philadelphia. He had another big fish to catch and gut out.

Chapter 32
Early The Next Morning
4th & Chestnut Streets

The famous Bourse Building was packed with locals and visitors from out of town. Lines of people stood around waiting to purchase food and souvenirs. Face and Private Investigator Vince Harris sat down at a small table. They decided to meet up at a public place and had a team of guards doing surveillance of the area.

"So have you got word yet," Vince asked. "Yes, I got a call last night from my source in Columbia," Face said. "You have to be extremely careful now. The C.O.U.P. is real and won't stop until you're a dead man," Vince warned. "I'm straight but what I need to know is who these people are," Face said. "There is more than just a few of them. They've been around for years and are connected to so many," Vince said. "Tell me what you know about these secret societies Vince," Face said.

The private investigator was worried that his associate was in grave danger. He knew the history and wanted Face to take as many precautions as possible; especially after's last night murder of Roberto Fuentes. He sat back in his chair and then he sat up straight and began to talk with Face.

"There's the C.O.U.P., The Trilateral Commission- which was founded by David Rockefeller in 1973. The C.F.R., which is short for the Council of Foreign Relations. They started back in 1921 and have headquarters in New York and D.C.; and they also publish a monthly journal called the Foreign Affairs. Then there's the Bilderberg Group which holds annual exclusive conferences for about one- hundred –and- twenty to one-hundred-and- forty members from North America and

Europe. They are people of power and influence, and they meet up at the Bilderberg Hotel in the Netherlands. It doesn't end there.

The Club of Rome, which started in 1968, has a location in Switzerland. The Committee of 300 is another one. They are also known as the Olympians. This is an international council which organizes politics, commerce, banking, media, and the military for centralized global efforts. Some of the other organizations under their influence are the N.A.A.C.P. and they have heavy ties to Harvard University. They are also in control of Wharton's School of Economics. Another name they go under is The Hidden Hand, which is headed by the powerful Rothschild family.

Some of the Committee of 300 members are Abdullah II, King of Jordon, Carl XVI Gustar, King of Sweden, Former President Clinton, David Rockefeller, and The British Royal family are in the clan as well. Their ultimate goal is establish a one world government with a unified church and monetary system. Better referred to as The New World Order," Vince ended.

Face sat there taking in the vast information he was just fed. He had heard many stories of the illuminati and of other secret societies, and often brushed them off or referred to them as another boogie-man tale. To have this information confirmed and to hear it firsthand, with dates of establishment, names of members, and their locations and ties to schools and organizations, gave them life. They were real. Face knew he was powerful but it was obsolete in comparison to the groups that were named.

"Damn, that's deep Vince. The world is truly controlled by a select few. While the wealthy continue to increase their reach and grasp on the world, the poor continue to dry up and die. We are nothing but mere puppets under their control and we don't even know it. They're building their own system and feeding us lies, as they trick us with fake images of wealth and freedom; when in fact we are all slaves under their system," Face said. "It's true. In fact Picasso said it best, an artist must discover the way to convince his public of the full truth of his lies," Vince said, as Face pondered over the quote.

"Just be careful Face. Keep your circle tight and watch those who watch. You have to handle your problem with the C.O.U.P. because with Roberto gone your name has just been moved up to the top of their list," Vince warned. "I'm not afraid. I was born for this and I believe God chose me to be his sword of mercy. Fear will not reside in me and I'm not going to allow them to implant any false realities in me either, "Face said, as he stood up and shook Vince's hand before walking away.

Chapter 33
One Week Later

Karen Brown knew all the ins and outs of the F.B.I.'s main office building. Being the personal secretary of the director had its advantages. She knew where all the confidential files were and how to access them, as well as knowing the director's weekly schedule. With that access she was able to get her hands on a file containing a list of paid informants, drug kingpins' profiles, and corrupt politicians. Her boss of six years had no clue that his trusted employee had been sleeping with the enemy; but she was turned out by Quincy, she loved him, and she would do anything for him.

Inside of the director's office Karen walked over to the large file cabinet and opened up the top drawer. She saw a yellow folder with the words "*Classified Information,*" written on it. While the director was out on his hour lunch, Karen opened the folder and started taking pictures of the file with her cellphone camera.

The sensitive information would be critical for Face's organization. The secret files contained information on Face, Reese, and details containing to their association with Roberto Fuentes. Also the names of Paul Warner and the late C.W. Watson were also written throughout the secret file. This file proved that the F.B.I., and A.T.F., along with other law enforcement agencies were trying to bring Face down. They had not given up the fight and as Karen took a photo of the bottom of one of the pages, she started to read it contents. It stated that Face was a terrorist and he, along with the members of his organization, should be terminated. Incarceration was not an option and it was signed by Paul Warner.

Karen quietly put away her phone and calmly walked out of the office. At that moment she realized the government was a part of an assassination to kill Face.

Manhattan, NY

Gloria Jones sat at her desk as she waited patiently. She had gotten a phone call a few hours earlier from the visitor she was now waiting on. Hearing the soft knock at the door, Gloria said, "Come in," as the door opened. Pamela walked inside and closed the door behind her.

"Have a seat," Gloria said, as she stood up and waited for Pamela to be seated before taking her seat. "It's good to see you," Pamela said, as she smiled at the beautiful woman. "Same here," Gloria replied.

Pamela's facial expression became serious as she turned her attention to the real reason she was there; and that wasn't for chit-chat and a cup of coffee. "I know about my grandson and I want to meet him," Pamela said to Gloria's surprise. "Face told you," she asked. "No, actually I overhead him talking about Samaj to his wife, so I decided to come see for myself. I need to meet my grandson. That's my flesh and blood," Pamela said in a demanding tone. "I'm fine with that Ms. Pam. I will tell him to come by here. School is out and he usually hangs out with a few friends, but I'll tell him to make his way over here," Gloria said.

Pamela was delighted. She wanted to meet the young man that was connected to her beloved son. Gloria watched the smile that danced on Pamela's face as she text Samaj.

Within an hour the young man had walked into his mother's law firm. The sight of Samaj's face brought tears to Pamela's eyes as she saw the uncanny resemblance. She rushed up and hugged the nervous young man. She didn't care that she had never met him before because this was her family. "I'm your grandmother," she said, as she pulled back from their hug and looked into his eyes. "You look so much like your father that it's a shame," she said. "It's nice to meet you," Samaj said, as he put out his hand for her to shake it. "Boy please," Pamela said, as she hugged him again. "I'm grandma, we don't play those games. We hug in this family," she said as she hugged him tighter.

Chapter 34
Later That Evening
Graterford Prison

Detective Roscoe Murphy needed a new snitch. He had been all throughout the streets of Philly looking for someone that had the scoop on Face and members of his crew. He had been to four Pennsylvania prisons but so far no one was willing to cooperate. Now as he sat at a small conference table at Graterford, he waited for the correctional officer to bring in an inmate.

When the door finally opened the CO's escorted a large man into the room. He was handcuffed and his feet were shackled with chains. "Thanks guys," Murphy said to the correctional officer as they sat the man down and exited the room. "Hi, Mr. Mathews," Murphy said. "What's up man? What do you want," the man said. "Well I'm here to help you…but that will depend on your willingness to help me," the detective said. "Help me with what," the man replied. "I can help you get ready to go home," Murphy said, as he opened up a folder.

"Your name is Nasir Mathews also known to many as Big Nas. I recently learned that you were celly's with Maurice Daniels; who goes by the name Reese. He's Face's right hand man," Murphy said. "What's that got to do with me," Nas said in an agitated and aggressive tone. "Calm down Mr. Mathews. Remember, I'm here to help you. You still have significant time to do behind stabbing that inmate a few months ago. Maybe I can get those charges dropped from your record," he said. "If I do what, snitch? Tell on some people or lie because you trying to build a case on Reese and Face," Nas said.

Detective Roscoe Murphy stood up from his chair and hovered over Nas. "Listen you asshole you're facing thirty years for attempted murder and you want to remember that when something sweet as this comes across your path. If you're willing to cooperate and tell me everything you know about Face and Reese, I'll make a few calls and have you out of here in seventy-two hours or less," Murphy pressed. Big Nas smiled at the detective. "Fuck you! Go find another nigga that's willing to cooperate. Now tell them nut ass CO's to take me back to my fuckin box," he said.

Big Nas was happy to return to his cell inside of the hole, where he was currently serving a 23 to 1 sentence. He was on twenty-three hour lockdown and only let out of his cell for an hour to exercise. As he sat on his cot he thought about his little homey Reese and the memories he had of him. Their card games and chess games had a lasting impression on him, and in just a few years they had formed a solid bond.

Reese was like a little brother to Nas and when Reese left the prison he still kept in touch. He wrote Nas often and money came monthly. As he sat reading his new favorite book, Young Rich and Dangerous, by Jimmy DaSaint, he laughed at the detective. He knew that many men would snitch at the drop of a dime to save themselves but Nas was loyal to his friend. He was a thorough breed.

West Philly

"Please! Please! Please," Marabella screamed out, as Doc fucked her savagely in the ass. Doc had her strapped down to the table and he pinned her down with his body as well. "Shut up you lying bitch! Just shut up," he said. "You're lucky I don't kill you," Doc exclaimed as he continued to torture her anus. The angrier he got as he thought about her escape, he began to choke her out. She was near unconsciousness as he felt her body going limp. Doc was pissed at his wife and wanted to fuck her until she couldn't move.

He let go of her neck and she began to gasp for air. She began to regain consciousness and then Doc began choking her again as he yelled, "If you ever leave me again I will kill you!"

Chapter 35
Later That Night
Cherry Hill, NJ

The large luxurious mansion was quiet. Face sent everyone over Veronica's while he prepared for Tasha's birthday. He needed some alone time with the woman he loved. With her eyes blindfolded, Face sung his own version of happy birthday, also rapping a verse where he declared his love for her, as he guided her into the living room.

"Can I take this off now," Tasha asked. "No, not yet. Give me a few more minutes," he said, as he helped Tasha sit down. "What are you up to Face," she asked, curious to see what he was doing. "You got so much patience, don't you? Just keep that blindfold on before I spank you," he said. "Oh, I might like that," Tasha giggled.

Tasha sat as calmly as she could. She could hear Face and another man whispering. Suddenly music from the stereo started to play. It was an instrumental from a song Tasha knew all too well. "Okay, take it off patience," Face said. When Tasha removed her blindfold she couldn't trust her eyes. Maybe they had been behind the blindfold to long because there was no way that her favorite singer, Eric Benet, was standing in her living room.

As Eric Benet began to sing Tasha's body trembled. Her husband had given her the ultimate gift and as the handsome singer serenaded her, tears of joy escaped from her eyes. Tasha even pinched herself a few times as she smiled at her loving husband, all while listening intently to Eric Benet.

"Thank you baby, I love you," Tasha mouthed to Face, as she continued to enjoy her birthday gift. Face had outdone himself and she was glad that he did.

Crowne Plaza Hotel
City Avenue

Karen's loud moans echoed throughout the private suite. Quincy had her up in his muscular arms as he fucked her with all he had. Like all the times before she was in pure bliss. Having sex with him never got old, and as an orgasms swept through her he could feel her body tremble, as her legs grew weak.

"Oh God! Oh God," Karen screamed, as Quincy pinned her back to the walk and started fucking her more aggressively. "Whose pussy is this," he demanded. "Yours Daddy! This is yours and only yours," she swore.

This was Quincy's way of thanking his loyal friend. The information she provided him was always needed and kept them on top of any upcoming and current investigations. Quincy promised that he'd make her pussy squirt endlessly for the recent information she had given him, and so far he had kept his promise.

Downtown Philadelphia

Inside of his hotel room, Paul Warner laid across his bed as he read the case files on Face's organization. Earlier that day he had been in D.C. to attend an important meeting with the C.O.U.P. to give the party updates on the current situation. He still had not known the exact whereabouts of Face but he managed to get an address on someone close to him; Veronica.

Paul knew Veronica was tied to the mysterious disappearance of agent Larry Sickler, and she was another target he would get to. The woman had knowledge about a few government officials' secrets and to him she was a threat. She had the power to bring down some men and crush their careers and reputations; and he was not going to allow that to happen. The President had already dismantled the Anti-drug commission after the death of Watson and he didn't want anyone going after Veronica over the rumored secret tapes, which could expose a scandal; so the C.O.U.P. knew they did not have The President's support if they went after her. If the tapes got released the people in them would be outcasts and they would be nothing more than has-beens; in a society where power and your name could bring you all your worldly desires.

Chapter 36
Center City

"Are you ready to leave," Kyle asked. "I'm so excited about tomorrow! I can't wait to get on that plane and leave this city," Arianna said. "I have too many bad memories in this city…way too many," she said, as she laid her head on Kyle's chest. "Our plane leaves at eight. I'll have a driver take us to the airport so we're not rushing," Kyle said. "That's great. Like I said, I can't wait to leave Philly behind. It's time to start building new memories," Arianna said, as Kyle rubbed her nearly noticeable pregnant belly.

Kyle thought about the city he loved and knew. Philly was his home but he could not risk the consequences of staying behind and disobeying Face's orders again. He knew he would not be given a second chance. As Arianna drifted off to sleep on his chest, he thought about their new life together and the joy he felt of becoming a first time dad. He would miss his home, the city of brotherly love that he knew like the back of his hand, but he had to set it free for his new family.

Cherry Hill, NJ

Face and Tasha stood in the doorway and watched as the soul singer Eric Benet waved goodbye and got into his waiting limousine. When the driver pulled off the coupled closed their door and walked up the stairs toward their bedroom.

"Thanks again baby. That was the best present ever," Tasha said, as the two entered the bedroom. "That was just an appetizer. I hope you're warmed up," Face said, as he kissed his wife on the nose.

The room was seductive and as the candles lit the air, and the rose peddles flowed on the bed and floor, Tasha's internal temperature rose as Face began to undress her. Tonight was going to be memorable and as he laid his beautiful wife onto the bed, she had a feeling this was going to be a long, enjoyable, and unforgettable night.

Early The Next Morning

At a private safe house located in South Philly, Face, Reese, and Quincy sat down as they talked about the recent discoveries and events that were facing them head on. Roberto Fuentes was dead but before his demise, he had shipped nine tones of pure cocaine to Philadelphia. It was all safely stashed away at a secret location on the outskirts of the city.

Face took a minute from speaking and then looked at both men and said, "After this shipment is gone, I'm done." Reese looked at him and said, "Done with what?" He knew what Face meant but he didn't know if he had been sure of his decision. "I'm done Reese. I want out. This ain't my game no more. It's not about the money because we have more than enough for generations to come," Face continued. "You always have to speak for me, right? I've never heard of anyone ever having enough money. The more you get the more you can do. I want to do it all. The money ain't slowed up so I don't know why you're trying to bounce," Reese said. "You'd lose your life while sitting on a billion dollars. That makes no sense to me Reese. I'm out," Face said. "I respect that Face. I think we've gotten to a place where we can do other ventures and still keep our heads," Quincy said. "So y'all teaming up on me now," Reese said. "We did this together and y'all just want to opt out."

Face looked at his friend and said, "Reese, when we started this we had a plan. We wanted to get rich, play the game our way, and never be labeled as snitches or be disloyal to the standing code. We've done that. We're beyond rich and we did this shit on our terms. And let's not forget that we promised to leave when we were on top. What position do you think we're in? We are definitely winning all the way around. It's our time to move on Reese."

Reese didn't want to leave the game. He loved it. It flowed through his veins and still gave him the same high as it did when they first started out.

"Reese, what's up? You're not gonna say nothing," Face asked, as Reese stood up and walked towards the door. "What can I say? You're the boss. You made the decision for all of us, right" Reese said sarcastically. "It's not like that and you know that. We brothers and I'm looking out for the family. The same men I walked in this with, I want them to be around when I walk out," Face pleaded. "I got work to do, if that's okay with you? I'll holla at y'all later," Reese said, as he walked out of the door.

Face walked to the window and watched Reese pull off. "Don't worry about Reese, that's your brother," Quincy said. "I just don't get him. He's got millions at his disposable and he still wants to be on some street time. Ain't no satisfying his hard-headed ass," Face said. "It's like they say, you can take the man out of the streets but the streets will always be in the man. Reese is a drug dealer and not a business man. He loves the game. Y'all two different kind of men. You held him down when he was in prison and when he got out all he had to do was get in line and help build the empire. The buildings built but he's not contempt. His heart is in the streets. He's aggressive and has a short temper. Reese is just that way, but he loves you. He's a man with his own way of thinking," Quincy said.

Face nodded his head. He was disappointed because the talk had not gone as he had planned. He knew Quincy was telling the truth and that truth may pose a problem to Face. That problem would be Reese. The two men had been close from childhood and there was nothing that separated them. He trusted Reese with his life and would give his for his brother. Together they had made millions, fought against Hood, the Gomez brothers, Truck, Ron Perry, and even the U.S. Government.

Face said goodbye to Quincy and got into his Porsche. He was hurting inside because he hated having disagreements with Reese. He felt off when things between the two of them were uneasy. As he drove off his mind was flooded with thoughts about where the two would stand as the dynamics of their relationship would have to change.

Chapter 37

Inside of Doc's dungeon of doom, Marabella and the crazed man sat at the kitchen table. A plate of fried rice and boiled eyeballs was in front of them. Doc had went out and killed a twenty-seven year old woman and got him some fresh eyeballs. Marbella sat calmly as she watched Doc place an eyeball inside of his mouth and swallowed it whole. Marabella couldn't stand the taste of human eyes in her mouth. It was so disgusting and every time she was forced to try them she would gag and throw up.

"What are you waiting for, eat up," Doc demanded. Marabella was afraid that if she didn't follow his directions after her failed escape that he would kill her, or worse. Since she had returned to the house Doc had become so volatile towards her. She didn't want to say or do the wrong thing, so she placed one of the eyes on her spoon and placed it into her mouth. As the overwhelming feeling to vomit emerged, she look at Doc's anger filled eyes and forced herself to swallow it.

Doc smiled at her like she was a dog who had just learned a trick he spent all week teaching and said, "See, not so bad." Marabella smiled but didn't respond. She hated Doc. The sight of him was sickening and he was a monster. She also hated Face for bringing this psycho into her life.

Her life as Peter J. Greenburg was no more. She was forced to smile pretty and pretend to enjoy Doc. She would not give up though because she could never accept this as her way of life. There was money for her to get to but she needed a way out of Philly, away from her capture. Marabella had millions of dollars stashed away and even after she gave Face the money from one of her accounts, she was nowhere near broke…but at the moment she had no way to get to it.

Pennsauken, NJ

Vince Harris sat down at this apple computer and went through all of his notes and records. He had already given Face all he had on a flash drive. Since Mike Conway's murder, Vince had been keeping tabs and studying the world's most powerful and secret societies. He was obsessed with how they operated and how they were able to stay under the radar for so long without detection.

While he attended Temple University he studied World History and Criminal Justice. That's where he first came across the mention of their existence. Vince was an intelligent and wise man who had stumbled upon a few secrets that same would kill for. The people in the society didn't mind outsiders discussing and passing their organizations off as rumors or urban myths, but if they knew the extensive research and data that Vince had on them; he may be their next target.

Paul Warner sat inside of his back Chrysler 300 as he looked through a pair of night-vision binoculars. Sitting a half a block away from his prey, he could see everything that was going on in front of Veronica's condominium. He had watched Veronica and two young children enter the building. Paul continued to watch as he noticed the two man security detail, that were dressed in plain clothing, as they sat in their car outside of her home.

Every half-hour one of the men would get out of the car and use a key to enter the home and check on

Veronica and the children. Paul had studied their moves and probed them for weaknesses. He was patient and as he drove away he knew he would be back soon to finish the job.

Chapter 38
6:23 P.M.
Center City, Philadelphia

Reese watched as Kyle got inside of his Lexus and drove off down the empty, dark street. Ever since Face had made the decision to spare Arianna's and Kyle's life, Reese had been watching them secretly. He knew today was their last day in Philly and once they left it would be unlikely that he'd ever see them again.

Dressed in all black, Reese put on his black leather gloves as he approached the home. The dark street was quiet and deserted. When Rese approached the front door he knocked twice and waited. He went inside of his pocket and pulled out a loaded .9mm. Suddenly the door opened and Arianna appeared with a shocked look upon her face. She thought Kyle had come back, but this man, who had a gun pointed at her, was nothing less than her worst nightmare.

Reese grabbed Arianna's long black hair as he pushed her into the house and slammed the door. He flung her onto the ground as she pleaded with him for mercy. She screamed out for help but her lips were silenced when Reese slapped her mouth with the tip of his gun. As she tasted the blood in her mouth from the busted-lip he had given her, she noticed that this man was Reese; Face's right hand man. She had seen his picture many times and knew his visit here would not end on a positive note.

"Bitch it's time for you to join the rest of your family," Reese said, as he aimed the gun at her chest and fired twice.

The bullets ripped through her chest as she lay on the floor struggling to breathe. Reese ran through the house, ransacking the place to make it look like a burglary.

While he was in other parts of the home, Arianna looked at the blood that was pouring from her chest and began to saturate her hands in her own blood. She struggled to write the letters to his name on the floor and was only able to write out the first three. The impact of her wounds proved to be to damaging to supply her hands with any more strength.

Reese continued to rush through the apartment as he came upon the pregnancy test on the dresser. He quickly picked it up and ran back to Arianna who was dying. He pulled his gun back out and aimed it directly at her and started to unloaded the rest of his clip into her unprotected stomach.

He calmly walked outside of the house, and his rage blinded him to the point that he did not see the message Arianna had left behind. As he climbed into his car he felt no remorse for the woman and unborn child he had just murdered. Reese was numb to his enemies and in his heart he had done Face a favor. He would never trust Kyle or Arianna and didn't want to take the risk of them returning to Philly and one day killing Face. He had to protect his brother because he knew Face was not thinking clearly lately.

In less than thirty minutes Kyle had returned. He had left for a minute to say a final goodbye to a few family members and friends. When he parked his car, he rushed back into the house to prepare for his family's departure. As he opened the door the horrific scene began to unfold as his pregnant fiancé lay on the floor in a pool of her own blood. Kyle knew a hit when he saw one and the bullets that littered his love's body made it clear this was not random.

He ran to her and held her close to him. There was nothing he could do for Arianna or the baby because they were gone. He felt empty and enraged as the tears of his reality rushed from his face. He noticed the letters *R,E,E,* written out in blood. It had been Arianna's final message and with just those three letters Kyle knew exactly who was behind this.

Chapter 39
Early The Next Morning
Washington, D.C.

Inside of the Oval Office, The President sat down at his desk as he went over the files his secretary had just given him. Moment later, Vice President Charles Bush entered the office and took a seat across from the President.

"Yes, Mr. President. You wanted to see me," he said. "I want to know who authorized the assassination of the Columbian drug lord, Roberto Fuentes? What the hell is going on Charles," he said.

Charles was shocked that the President had found out that information. He was clearly exposed. "Sir, I did," he said, as he waited on The President's response. "Where do you get off authorizing assassinations without my permission," he said, demanding a meaningful response. "No disrespect Sir but we both know that Roberto Fuentes needed to be eliminated. He was one of the top suppliers of cocaine and heroin in the states. How long could we have allowed him to continue?"

The President stood up and walked in front of The VP. "I know what's going on and I don't like it. I know all about this hit and several other unofficial covert missions you ordered. I don't think you understand the chain of command! You are not the President, I AM," he shouted.

"The American people made their choice and I am here to uphold the oath I made to this office. You're running around like a street gangster and have clearly lost your senses. The law is not bent for you and the murders you've participated in are on your hands. This is my term, this is my term, and you will fall in line," The President demanded.

The VP nodded his head in agreement but he didn't care what The President had said. Charles was a member of the C.O.U.P. and if he wanted to he could arrange the assassination of The President in less than 48 hours. However, he knew the heat behind it could ruin him so he had to play ball.

"I don't want to make this a bigger issue than it has to be Charles. I have always respected you and want to keep it that way but this happens no more. Nothing happens without my permission." The VP stood up from his chair and said, "Sir, I will fix things now. This won't happen again," he said, as he walked out of the office.

The President may have thought he had an impact on The VP but that wasn't the case. The next assassination was already in the works. Paul Warner was in Philadelphia waiting to make his move.

Downtown Philadelphia

Face sat down across from his new accountant as he read through his financial statements. An hour earlier he was signing off on some important documents. Face was making sure that all his personal business was in complete order. He owned corporations all across America and Canada, and he even had a few in different regions of Mexico.

"Looks real good Samual. Did Tasha get a copy of this," Face asked. "Yes, Mr. Smith. I sent it to her by email less than an hour ago," he said. "Great," Face said, as he continued to read through his files.

Face made bi-weekly visits to his accountants and financial advisors because he promised himself he would never allow his past to revisit him. Peter J. Greenburg had taught him never to trust anyone with his money, so he was very proactive about going over his files. He wanted to know where every dime was coming from and where it was going.

Samual Reinstein was one of the top CPA's and financial advisors on the east coast. His company represented some of the wealthiest people in the world and it was his job to protect their assets, which he did an excellent job at. Tasha and Face were two of his biggest clients and he found them new ways to make money and better yet, the best way to hide it.

"The plane will be ready for the trip out to the Cayman's. The money will be there too. The same amount as last time right," Samual asked. "Yes, a ten million, "Face said, as he sat the file on the desk. "Okay Mr. Smith, I've got everything taken care of. The money will be deposited into your account, and then I'll have it wired back to that States into your corporations. The bank president is already willing to play ball. Plus he don't care what we do as long as he gets his twelve percent," Samual laughed.

Before Face could respond, his cell phone rung. "What's up Q," he asked. "The chick is dead," Quincy said. "What chick," Face asked. "Hood's daughter. She was shot over ten times and the shit is all over the news," Quincy said frustrated. "Damn, just meet me at the spot," Face said, ending the call.

The accountant watched as his client's mood had gone from upbeat to straight downhill. "Are you okay Mr. Smith," Samual asked. "No. Just take care of the money. I have to go," Face said as he grabbed his jacket and rushed out of the door.

"Reese, what the fuck have you done," Face said to himself, as he made his way to his Bentley. He tried calling Reese's phone but got no answer, as he rode in the back of his car. He was furious. He told Reese to walk away from the situation but he went against his orders. Face tried calling him a few more times but he got the same response as when he first called. Face was pissed and not about the girl's death. She had tried to kill him but once he had made the decision Reese should have respected him. In all the years they had been partners it was the first time Reese had ever disobeyed a direct order from him. Face had to take several deep breaths to calm down.

"Are you okay boss," the driver asked, as he turned the limo down Chestnut Street. "No, just drive," Face said, as the man continued on to his destination.

Face stared out of the window as he continued to try and calm himself. His cell phone rang and he rushed to answer it because it was Reese finally retuning his call. "Where are you," Face asked. "I'm in Atlantic City with my girl and my daughter," Reese replied. "Get back to Philly now we need to talk," Face demanded. "I'm.," Face interrupted him. "I'm not asking you shit, get back now! I'll be waiting in my main spot."

Face ended the call and quickly dialed another number. On the third ring the phone was answered.

"Hello."

"Kyle are you okay? I heard what happened."

"I'm good Face. I'm good."

"Don't lie to me. Are you good or not?"

"…Face she was pregnant. She was pregnant with my first born! I'm okay. I'm going to bury them next to her brother. She would have wanted that."

Face could feel the pain bleeding in Kyle's voice as he delivered the news. Face was saddened by the entire situation and surely wouldn't have killed a pregnant woman. The more Face thought about the situation he knew the game had run its course. He had to get out before he lost someone close to him; or even his own life.

Chapter 40
Center City, Philadelphia

Detective Roscoe Murphy stood outside of Arianna's condo watching as the two paramedics rolled her lifeless body out on a gurney. Police officers had the block taped off as the yellow caution tape signaled a fatally had occurred. Reporters from all the local TV stations were present as they tried to squeeze out as many details they could about the homicide. The tragic death of a college student was big news, and detective Murphy had known more about the case than he led on. He knew the victim and he had known her family. Many years ago Arianna's mother had been his unit sergeant, and Robbie's death was one of his cold case files. There was nothing random about this case. Arianna had been murdered and he knew there was a bigger motive than a simple robbery gone badly.

As the body headed towards the morgue, Detective Murphy searched the home for telling signs of how the crime unfolded. He noticed immediately that there was no forced entry. She had either known her killer or been caught off guard. The house had been processed for fingerprints and none were there that didn't belong. When he walked over to the spot where Arianna had been murdered, he saw the blood crusted letters R,E,E, that had been written out. He made sure the CSI tech on the scene had photographed that clue.

On his way out of the door, the tech handed him the positive pregnancy test he had found on the floor. Murphy took out his cellphone and placed a call.

"What's up Murphy," a male's voice said. "I'm on my way to the Coroner. The deceased female was possibly pregnant, so we may have a double homicide on our hands," Murphy said. "Okay, I'll let them know you're on the way," the man said, as they hung up with each other.

Walking to his car, Detective Murphy was enraged. "Face, you couldn't rest until you got the whole family you son-of-a-bitch," he said as he got into his car.

Belmont Plateau
Fairmont Park, West Philly

Before Kyle left Arianna's place he removed all of his clothes and possessions. He was sure to wipe everything off in lye to erase any trace of him being in the home. Quincy and Kyle had cleaned up a few murder scenes before and even though it was emotionally troubling, he was able to get the job done.

Kyle sat in his parked car as he thought about the short time he had spent with Arianna, and how loving her had made him feel alive. There was no amount of words or prayer that could console his broken heart. He had not only loss the woman he loved but the child he was eager to parent had been killed as well. Reese had cut him deep and all he could do was ball up in his car and let the tears of anguish fall from his eyes.

Buddakan Restaurant
3rd & Chestnut Streets

Frank "Underworld" Simms sat at his table with his partner Craig reading the Daily News. The headline said: Temple student Gunned Down Inside of Her Home, and all Underworld could do was shake his head. He knew the real story behind the one the media had put out. He was well aware of the biological relationship between Hood and Arianna; and that she was the last living member of

Hood's legacy. As well as the hatred Face and Reese shared for Hood. Underworld had heard the rumors about Face having Hood's heart removed, and even though no one had proof, they knew Face was behind the death of Hood and his entire family.

Underworld sat the paper down in an empty seat next to him and looked up at Craig. "Damn, the whole family got wiped out," he said, as he scooped up a spoonful of soup. "Yeah, it's an ugly game out here. Definitely not for everyone," Craig said, as he took a piece of his salmon. "You can't leave no enemy behind," Craig continued, as he chewed on his moist fish. "Yeah, I guess not. At least you know they're not coming back for you," Underworld said. "There's a lesson in this. You have to be willing to take out your enemies no matter the cost; unless you want them to come back for you. Loved ones aren't off limits and if you want to survive this dirty game you've gotta be all in,' Craig said.

Chapter 41
Belmont Avenue
West Philadelphia

When Reese walked into the secret stash house and Face was already sitting down at the table waiting on him. Reese walked over to Face and joined him as he sat in the empty chair. Face didn't speak initially; instead he stared at Reese with a look of disgust directed towards him. He didn't know where to start the conversation because he was still trying to understand why Reese had killed Arianna. At times Reese and Face were like brothers. He was like his other half. Then there were those other times when their relationship felt distant and empty.

"What's up Face," Reese said, trying to avoid the awkward silence. "Why Reese? Why did you kill that girl," Face asked. Reese looked directly at his friend and said, "Because it needed to be done. I did it for you." Face was fuming. Why was Reese such a hot head? He was tired of his crap. "Listen, you did it for you and probably because I told you not to. The girl was pregnant and you had no rights to fuck with her," Face said. "No rights! I made a promise to you when I was younger that I'd have your back. You said you would have mine too and what I did was for you! I had your back because I know you can't trust nobody who pulled a gun out on you and had the heart to pull the damn trigger," Reese exclaimed.

"I made it clear she was to be left alone but you disobeyed that. If you wanted to have my back then you should have listened to what I said. I did not get us here by luck. I use my fucking brain and made tough decisions that have moved us up the ladder and kept us out of harm's way the best I could! I used my brain and it wouldn't hurt if you used yours a bit more! Now you got a potential enemy that we didn't have before," Face said.

"Face I'm not worried about Kyle! He's nobody to me. He violated and he ought to be glad that I didn't kill him too. He had a job to do and instead of handling our problem he makes a new one and falls in love with that bitch. That's Hood's daughter. Let's call her what she is. She ain't some regular chick! She was coming to kill you and if she ever found out from that soft ass nigga Kyle who he really was, what would have stopped her from coming back to finish the job she started," Reese said.

"You feeling yourself! Good because I'm done with this shit! After this shipment clears out I'm done with it. I've been on the paper chase for too long and I got what I came in this game to get. I'm not going to lose myself and I'm not about to run around the streets shooting people like I'm still a hungry ass young-bull," Face said.

After a few moments of silence, Reese stood up from his chair and said, "Face I love you like a big brother but if you decide to walk, that's your decisions. It won't be mine. This game is what I know; it's what I love and leaving ain't an option." Face looked at Reese and said, "Well after this shipment is clear we go our separate ways because my life is more than this game. I have a family and that's more important to me than playing this game of cops and robbers with you." Reese replied, "Well that's what it will be and ain't no sorry's up in me for taking care of that girl. I did you a favor. I guess I love my homey too much," Reese said, before he turned from Face and walked out of the door.

Four Days Later

Inside of the beautiful Mount Laurel cemetery, Kyle stood a few feet away from Arianna's burial plot. He had just watched as the fresh dirt was laid over her white casket. She had been buried just a few feet away from her mother, brother, and father. There was an eerie silence on the grounds and the only guests there to pay their respects were Kyle and the minister. The gloomy skies covered them as the pastor said a final prayer.

Once the pastor said his goodbyes, he left Kyle at the gravesite alone. Kyle stood in silence as he tried to wrap his mind around the reality of his situation. He had just been with this woman. He had just made love to her and they were excited to be moving away from this city that had brought his fiancé so much pain. As he sat there reflecting, he heard a car pull up not too far away from where he was standing. He watched as Face got out of his Bentley and made his way towards him.

Face hugged Kyle and placed a dozen red roses near the open grave of the young woman had who tried to kill him. He didn't allow that fact to keep him from being there for a friend. Even though it made no sense and the entire situation could have been avoided if Kyle would have followed orders, none of that mattered. What mattered was that his friend needed some support.

"Love you Lil Homey, I'll see you soon. Don't take off, okay," Face said, as he walked away and returned back to his car. Kyle never questioned Face as to how he knew where he was, because there wasn't much that Face didn't know. He was too well connected. All that mattered to him was that someone other than himself had come and paid Arianna some respect. Kyle had always had the utmost respect for Face and his act of kindness showed his true character.

Chapter 42
8:45 P.M.
Center City, Philadelphia

Like a hawk eyeing its prey, Paul Warner watched Veronica closely. He had been patiently waiting for the perfect moment to make his move and the moment had finally arrived. As the sky grew dark, Paul grabbed his .9mm and quickly screwed on his silencer. He was dressed in all black and with the faded light; he began to blend into the night.

Paul exited his vehicle that was parked a block away and made his way closer to his target. He clutched his pistol tightly as he held it in his hand, and he continued walking towards the Dodge Mangum that was just a few feet away from him. Inside sat two of Face's security team members who were detailed to provide protection and security for Veronica.

Sneaking up on the car he saw the men were smoking in the vehicle. They had their windows rolled down as they blew their marijuana smoke into the night. Without warning Paul took precise aim and squeezed the trigger, firing four silent but lethal shots into the men's heads. He went into the pocket of the man who had the keycard to the building and quickly retrieved it from his possession.

Paul walked away from the car and towards the condo. He keyed his way into the building with no problems and made his way towards Veronica's condo. Paul knew the exact time that the men would check on Veronica, so he knocked on the door and waiting for her to answer.

As the door opened Veronica expected to see the security detail but instead she was met by Paul Warner, who was pointing his gun directly at her. Standing in her all white rope, Veronica was shocked and clearly shaken as her body began to shiver.

"Turn around," Paul demanded as he walked behind Veronica with his gun pointed at the back of her head. Fear swept throughout her body as she followed his commands and quietly prayed for a way out. Without uttering another word Paul shot Veronica in the back of her head, wounding her fatally, as her body fell to the floor. Brain matter had been discharged from her head and now, like her security detail outside, she was no more. Her past had finally caught up to her.

Calmly and slowly, Paul walked out of the door. The man had never noticed Suri, who had come out of her room to find her godmother. As she walked closer to her slain guardian, she froze and the tears ran from her face as she saw the blood and mangled head of Veronica laid out on the floor. She had never seen any violence in her young life. Suri was very protected and had never even watched a movie that wasn't age appropriate; but in this moment the young child's life had been changed as the reality of her father's lifestyle came crashing at the door.

Cherry Hill, NJ

Veronica's death crushed Face and his family, and the news of the triple homicide spread through the city like wildfire. Many of Veronica former clients who were out on Capitol Hill got word of her death too, and they became worried. The secret tapes she held had kept her protected and now that she had been murdered, they worried about the whereabouts of those tapes.

Face's intuition told him that Paul Warner and the C.O.U.P. were behind the murder, as he sat with his wife and mother as they all grieved. Pamela was inconsolable, as the tears poured from her eyes and her nose ran like a broken faucet. She had lost her best friend and sister. Veronica had been her go to person when times got tough, and she had always been there for her family. She was the one person that Pamela could share her fears and secrets with. Her head ached as she stood up and then collapsed to the floor trying to process the fact that she would never see her sassy, sexy, loving, funny, witty and charming best girlfriend every again.

The family had suffered a loss and Face was outraged. Veronica was his aunt, and he wanted to see her around until her hair was grey, her legs were weak, and her heart got so old that it would no longer beat; but Paul had snatched her away from him…and he destroyed Suri's innocence in the process. His young daughter would not stop crying and in her fragile state they didn't know what they could say to her to help. Tasha held her baby girl and tried to comfort Suri as she fought back the pain that weighed her down. Veronica and Tasha shared a bond as well. The years they had known each other and the obstacles and challenges the family had faced, did nothing but strengthen them. The score had to be settled.

Reese and Quincy rushed over to Face's as the news reached them. They were hurt but trying to be strong for their friend and his family. Both men's eyes were filled with tears as they entered the home and stood in shock. They had never seen the family broken and neither knew what to do or say. As Face stood up, his eyes were red and sore, and his knees buckled as he headed towards the kitchen. Reese and Quincy followed behind him.

"I don't want to do no more talking! I want them dead! All those motherfuckers have to pay and I don't care how much! They killed Veronica," he said, as he slumped onto the large kitchen's island and purged. "Don't worry Face, we will take care of this," Quincy said, as he walked over to his friend and placed his hand on his shoulder. Reese paced back and forth, as he angrily contemplated a move. He was enraged and just wanted to shoot somebody. The family had lost another member and it was killing them.

"They killed one of us and now they've got to lose ten," Face said, as he stood up and punched the countertop. "They killed one of us and now we kill a hundred of theirs. No mercy, no talk, no regrets. I need us to handle this," Reese said, as he walked up to his friend and brother and embraced him.

Chapter 43
Center City, Philadelphia

Detective Roscoe Murphy couldn't understand what was happening on the streets of Philly. In less than two months over fifteen homicides had taken place in the City of Brotherly Love; and based on his sources the deaths could be all linked to Face's organization if the right pieces of the puzzle could be tied together.

As he parked his car across from Veronica's condo he looked out his window at the F.B.I. agents on the scene. The Feds had taken over the criminal investigation and it was the first time Deceive Murphy had seen anything like this. This case was much bigger than it appeared and he wanted to know why the Feds were all up in his backyard.

"What's going on," he said to himself, as he watched the men on the scene. The Police Department had enough man power to tackle this case and the detectives had the training and skill to solve it, so why were the Feds all over it. "Excuse me but you're going to need to move. This is a closed scene," the Federal Agent said. "No problem. Could you tell me what's going on? Why are the Feds here," Detective Murphy asked. "We are not authorized to discuss that with you, I'm sorry. So if you'd just go I have to clear this area," the agent said, as Detective Murphy started up his car.

As he pulled down the street, his sixth sense was telling him he needed to do some digging. He had to find out why the Feds were on this case. It was a homicide and his division could have worked the case, so why they were pushing his crew away made no sense. There was something missing and things didn't pan out. He had to know what was really happening behind those walls.

Inside of Veronica's condo F.B.I. agents searched every room for the secret tapes. The Vice President had sent a special team to Philly to conduct a thorough search so he could get his hands on the priceless tapes. They had been given strict instructions to keep the mission private and to turn up every stone until they found the precious videos.

The agents spent several hours searching and continued to come up empty handed. They read through her daily notepad and found nothing but a basic to do list. They had no clues as to where else they could look, as they went over the place with a fine toothed comb. The only thing of value was a suitcase full of cash under her bedroom, and they confiscated a few personal photos of Veronica and her friends. The agents were still empty handed because the tapes were their platinum and the search didn't even produce a bronze medal.

Later That Evening
Washington, D.C.

The President was heated about the troubling news he had just received. Within just a few hours of Veronica's death, he had been informed about the incident. He had people in his cabinet looking into the actions of his VP because he knew he could not trust him. He instructed The Vice President to put a stop to these unapproved hits but with the new file sitting on his deck it was apparent his VP was not following instructions.

The President comprised a team of U.S. Marshalls that kept him abreast of the happenings going around. Even though he was the Chief, there were so many people plotting and making moves that he needed to be aware of. The government was filled with shady characters who were all working for their own interest. Congressman,

Senators, and member of the House of Representatives all had their own agenda's. In the U.S. capital it was nothing but a dog-eat-dog type of world.

Vice President Charles Bush had been urgently summoned and now he walked calmly through the doors of the oval office. As he closed the door behind him he was met by the angered President. "What the hell happened in Philadelphia," he asked. The VP walked close towards the President as they stood face to face. "Mr. President we need to get something clear here. You don't run anything and we both know that! You made good with some powerful people and they helped you get here; and some members of my party supported you but you don't run anything," Vice President Charles Bush said.

The President of The United States took a step back and listened in silence as The VP continued. "This is your first term and you'll be lucky if you get another go around. We might allow that and we might not. You will never have the power you think this office holds and we both know that the last President to have full control of this office was Roosevelt. I guarantee you those days are long gone."

The President responded, "I don't appreciate the way you're speaking to me." The VP pointed his finger at The President and said, "We both know it's not a damn thing you can do about it. I can make a phone call and your wife and children can disappear before dinner." The President snapped, "Are you threatening me, Charles?"

Vice President Charles Bush walked closer to The President. He placed his lips to The President's ear and said, "No nigger, I'm telling you." Then he turned away and walked out of the door, leaving, theoretically, the most powerful man in the country, The President of the United States, speechless.

Chapter 44
Later That Night
Downtown

Two sets of eyes watched as Paul Warner got out of his car and walked into the lobby of the Drake hotel. "He's on his way up," one of the men who had been watching Paul said into his cellphone. The men had been eagerly waiting for Paul to return to his hotel and it had been several hours before he returned. Three hotel employees had been paid five thousand dollars each for their cooperation and silence for the evening; and even the hotel's security manger had been paid to erase their entry to the building and to stop all recordings until they had left.

Paul entered the elevator and pressed the button to take him to the third floor. Since his stay in the hotel he had his room changed twice just so that no one would know his direct location. He didn't trust anyone besides his brothers and sisters of the C.O.U.P. and the added precautions made him feel as comfortable as he could.

"Third Floor," the prerecorded voice said as the elevator doors opened and he walked off. He walked to suite 315 and took out his keycard and went inside. The room was filled with darkness as he reached for the light switch to give him sight. With a click of the switch the room was lit but to his surprise there was new scenery in his room. Quincy, Reese, and Face stood just a few feet away from Paul Warner.

Their guns were loaded and ready to send slugs through the man's body who had ruptured their hearts. As Reese took aim at Paul's head, Face said, "We know who you are Paul and we know who you work for. You're not the only one who can find people and put an end to them.

We have eyes all over this city and right now I want to introduce myself to you. I know this is not the meeting you thought we would have. You thought you'd be looking through your scope and within seconds you'd be bragging to the C.O.U.P. about how you took me out. No, you won't be having that conversation. You fucked up. What's going to happen now will be different than what you're used to. It will be worse than the pain you felt when you lost your arm; it will be the worse pain you ever felt in your life."

Suddenly Doc walked out of the bedroom and into the common space of the hotel room. He was carrying a large briefcase and a small wooden stool. "Sit down," Doc said to Paul. "And make sure you guys keep your eyes on this fella, I'm sure he has a weapon or two on him," Doc said to the men.

Paul sat on the stool as Reese removed the gun he had on his waist and another gun he had strapped to his ankle. Face was in total rage and he had never hated another man as much as he hated Hood, until today. "Y'all will never get away with this. We are too powerful and they won't rest until all of you are dead," Paul shouted out. He was used to killing and had said many times that he would show no fear if death knocked at his door. However, his prior words didn't match his current situation because when death is staring you in the face even the toughest alive will be brought to their knees.

Doc grabbed a roll of silver duct tape from out of his briefcase and wrapped it around Paul's mouth. Then he handcuffed his legs and one arm to the stool. Face walked over to Paul and said, "Enjoy what you have given to so many because I'm going to enjoy every minute of this." Paul's face began to quiver as he struggled to hold his composure. He had been caught totally off guard and he knew pleading for his life and begging would not change his current impending fate.

Doc removed a large machete from his briefcase and passed it to Face. Then Reese walked over to Paul and grabbed his head and held it steady. Paul tried to twitch but Reese's grip was firm and unshakeable. His neck was in full view and when Face swung the large knife, he almost sliced his entire head off. The pain of being beheaded alive squealed from Paul's eyes, as Reese grabbed his head again so Face could take another swipe. Blood gushed as Face swung the sharp knife and cut bone. He began to saw his neck off as Paul's body shake and twitched, as his eyes rolled into the back of his head. Face's rage showed as he sawed through bone like he had been simply cutting a piece of beef.

With Paul's head off and his dead body still attached to the chair, the men began the cleanup while Quincy searched the hotel for any information that might be useful to them. He didn't find anything helpful so he began to help the men clean up the scene. When they had removed all traceable evidence, Face and Reese changed out of their bloody clothing and then exited the hotel as calmly as they had entered.

A waiting Philadelphia Police car was waiting for them as the men exited a rear door. Face sat up front with the officer, and Doc, Reese, and Quincy got into the back of the car. The officer drove them to an enclosed garage on Washington Avenue and the men all got out of the car. The officer, who was on Face's payroll, drove away and he was paid half of his yearly salary for the escort.

The men got into their individual cars and went away in separate direction. Reese headed South, Quincy was going North, Doc returned to his home in West Philly, and Face headed to his family in Jersey. The death of Paul

Warner was on Face's mind as he crossed the Ben Franklin Bridge. He wanted the man dead but he was not satisfied. There was nothing that could heal the wound that the loss of Veronica brought. As Face drove off the memories he shared with Veronica began to flood his brain. His eyes grew heavy as the flashback of her smile broke his heart all over again. The family was broken and he didn't know if time could heal this pain. There was a gaping wound in his heart and he struggled with his pain, as he fought back his tears and made his way back home.

Chapter 45
Three Days Later
Washington, D.C.

The members of the C.O.U.P. sat around the large table in disbelief. Their number one assassin had been found decapitated inside of his private suite in a luxury Philadelphia hotel. The Feds had an all-out investigation in full swing because they had to find out who had murdered Paul Warner. They crime scene was clean and there was nothing from the room that could be used to track the killer or killers; and the Feds were even more dumbfounded when they found out the security system had been experiencing technical difficulties and the cameras had no useful footage.

The members of the secret society were outraged. One of their own had been touched and they wanted answers. Charles Bush knew that Face was responsible so he immediately assigned a team to track him down and kill him, along with his entire family. Charles had never gotten over the death of his lover Watson and now Face had gotten rid of his top-gun and he wanted revenge.

Vice President Charles Bush stood up from the table and said, "We will find out who took our brother from us. I have a team in Philadelphia now and they will not rest until I have his head! I am going to get to the bottom of this, I promise you all that." Everyone stood up from the table and raised their right hands in the air. Their shiny gold-nugget member rings adorned their pinky fingers as they said in unison, "To our brother Paul, may he rest peacefully; and until we see you again when it's our turn to enter the dark world!"

The VP addressed the members as they took their seats. "In three days we will go on our annual vacation without our brother. He will be in there in spirit and his murderers will be brought to justice," he said, as the members began to cheer and lift their right hands back into the air to proceed with their next chant. "We control the lives of the people in this country. We control the world," he shouted as the room erupted with cheers. Their society had been around for over a hundred years and their power stretched deep; and it was their quest to stay in power as long as human beings lived on this earth.

West Philly

Doc and Marabella sat at the table as they ate some brown rice, sautéed tongue and ears, and the eyeballs; which all came from Paul Warner. Doc was rewarded the head of Paul Warner after the kill and just like he had promised Face, he would get rid of each part. Doc had felt the pain that his friends were going through due to the loss of Veronica, so it was an honor for him to further torture Paul's legacy by eating him. Anyone who was an enemy of Face would always be one to Doc.

Detective Roscoe Murphy pulled his car into the driveway of the vast and beautiful estate. He placed his car in park and removed the key, as he got out and walked up to the front door. When he rang the bell he waited as he heard the approaching footsteps. A short, older Spanish woman opened the door and invited the detective inside. "The Judge is waiting for you," she said. He followed behind the woman as she led him into the living room. The older Caucasian man, with a head full of grey, was sitting on his sofa reading the Philadelphia Daily Newspaper.

"How are you Judge Kauffman? It's nice to see you again," Detective Murphy said. "Have a seat detective. I was enjoying my newspaper and then you walked in. So what is it this time, what do you want," the grumpy old Judge asked. "Well, after reading over the transcripts for Face's trial, and going over so many statements, and other evidence from the Prosecution there is no way that man should have been acquitted. With the informants testimony alone he should have been serving life right now. I just don't understand how a mistake like this could happen; especially with a case as high profile as this?"

Judge Kauffman sat his newspaper down and shot Detective Murphy a look that could cut. He had presided over the trial and had put that case behind him. He knew the particulars all too well, and now to have this prying detective bringing up a closed cased made his pressure rise. All he wanted to do was enjoy his retirement and live out the last of his glory days in his beautiful home on his Conshohocken estate.

"It was out of my hands and the jury made their decision. That man was powerful and his reach may have been longer than what anyone in the courtroom could have imagined. We all knew he was one of the biggest drug dealers in the U.S., and he proved to be untouchable during that trial," the judge said. Detective Murphy felt he may have been on to something so he kept digging. "But with the testimony alone of the Gomez Brothers he shouldn't have walked. That was the smoking gun. How could anyone look facts in the face and get a pass? The system can't be that screwed up."

Judge Kauffman looked at Detective Murphy and unloaded a secret he had been carrying around for some time. He had known in his heart the verdict was unjust and he was a man of the law; and today he wanted to unload some truths.

"It was Veronica. She got Face off?"

"Who is she?"

"The woman who was murdered in her condo along with her two bodyguards, that's Veronica. She's close to Face, their like family?"

"Well how could she help him get off?"

"She was a top escort in the city with some very high profile clients. Many who were connected to the law as well as those who had political ties? She had the power to bring down a lot of people and she used that power to help him. When they came after Face she knew what she had to do to save him."

"Well damn. You're telling me a high price whore had the power to get him off because she had sex with some important people?"

"No, it's more than some damn names. She had tapes of everyone she had ever had sex with. She recorded us secretly and no one knew she was taping them."

"You said us? You slept with her too," the detective asked, causing the judge to pause before responding.

"Yes, I am guilty of having sex with the woman. She was my mistress but I never thought she was recording me. She threatened to send those tapes to all the media outlets and you can imagine the humiliation that would have caused. Not to mention many people would have lost their careers and credibility. Families would have been crushed. She was out for blood and those damn tapes would have ruined us if they had gotten out. "

"So who decided that he would be acquitted, you?"

"No, I'm still a small fish in that pond. The call came from the boys out in Washington. The Vice President and

Senator Watson paid me a visit and gave me the order to have the man acquitted."

"So what happened to the tapes?"

"Nobody knows. She never released them and they haven't been heard of since she threatened to go public with them."

"I think that's what the Feds were looking for in her condo."

"Well, we can be sure they were looking for them if they don't have their hands on them. No one can risk having those tapes leaked. You need to know this information I'm telling you can't be leaked either. You're not a damn reporter so don't do anything stupid. If you can't get to Face through your own means, then you might be wasting your time. He's connected and if those tapes are out there he might be untouchable, especially if he has them in his possession."

Chapter 46
Three Next Day

Tasha tried her best to go on with her normal routine but Veronica's tragic death weighed heavily on her mind and heart; so much so that she often found herself dazed and unable to remember what she had been trying to do. When she headed into work there was a serious detail of security following her. Face was not taking any chances; even with Paul Warner gone he was not going to allow anyone to hurt his family, so she was being escorted by armed guards wherever she went.

Face had purchased a bullet proof car for Tasha and she was driven around by an armed driver; and there also was an armed guard who rode inside of the car with her. Behind her she was followed by a car full of men who were ready to shoot and kill any threats if they arose.

While Tasha was being driven into work, no one paid attention to the helicopter that had been high above them. The men inside had been ordered to keep a tail on her. The co-pilot pulled out his cellphone and made a call. "Sir, we have her in sight." The person on the other end said, "Good, just keep an eye on her until I get to Philadelphia," as he hung up and the line went dead.

Private Investigator Vince Harris was sitting at his desk when he got a call. He had just found out through a credible source that C.O.U.P. member Paul Warner had been killed and beheaded. He searched the internet for any news on the murder but just as he suspected there was none. The organization would not allow the details of their top assassin's death to be plastered over the web. They would do their best to cover it up, the same way they covered up the assassination of President John F. Kennedy. Concealment was another one of their powers, along with the power to dictate what truths the news media's put out. This organization was the puppet master and for so many years the public had been none the wiser.

Vince turned off his computer and sat back in his chair. Face had taken care of a mutual enemy when he killed Paul Warner and Vince was very pleased. The death of Paul Warner and his beheading had been the best news he had heard all day.

Later That Evening
Cherry Hill, New Jersey

Pamela lay across her bed as she stared at a picture of Veronica. It was a picture they had taken fifteen years ago, while they were out at a nightclub in downtown Philly. She had lost a sister and the tears flowed steadily from her eyes as she wished this had all been a bad dream. The pain she felt was indescribable as this stabbing pain constantly erupted in her belly.

Her sister's funeral was tomorrow and she didn't feel as though she had the strength to go. She screamed out as she lay in her bed crying. She ached and she felt empty, as she cried into the darkness.

Cayman Islands

The 60XR Lear Jet landed safely on the runway. When the doors swung open, Samual Reinstein stepped off of the jet as he held a large briefcase. Behind him four men carried two briefcases each as they headed towards the van. A black limousine moved closer to the plane and parked. Then a slim man quickly got out.

"How are you? How was your flight Mr. Reinstein," he asked. "I slept the whole way so it had to be great," Samual replied, as the two laughed. The men stood side by side as the four men crew loaded up the van with the briefcases filled with the large quantity of U.S. currency that was in their hands and on the plane.

"How is Mr. Smith doing today," the man asked Samual. "He's fine, at home with the family," Samual replied. "That's great. His money is safe down here with us," the man said. "We know that and he appreciates that it is."

After the men had finished loading the limousine with up with the briefcases filled with cash, the crew got back onto the plane. Then Samual and Larry got inside the limousine and drove off as the van followed behind. Larry Kutcher was the President of the Cayman Island International Bank. He had held that position for eight years and was making a pretty penny off the 12% fee he charged all of his clients.

"Is Mr. Smith still interested in owning property down here," Larry asked. "That would be a great investment for him. I'll go over it with him when I get back to the states and see what he wants to do, but right now I have to keep my focus on depositing these millions," Samual said, as he took a puff of his Cuban cigar.

Chapter 47
9:13 A.M.
Northeast Philadelphia

Inside of the Garden of Angels private cemetery family and friends stood around as Veronica's gold colored casket was placed into the cold ground. Tears escaped many of the onlookers' eyes, as others hugged each other and did their best to be strong as Veronica was lowered into her final resting place.

High above them Face heard and saw a helicopter as it flew pass, but he wasn't alarmed by the chopper. He had men on the grounds that were ready and able to light up anyone whose presence was not welcomed. Face's family was out in full sight and the men he had hired knew that even though this was a funeral, protection of his family was their number one assignment.

Pamela was having a hard time standing as she buckled and cried out in anguish. She had never felt so weak and she was dehydrated from all of the crying she had done. Tasha did her best to comfort her but her best was not good enough. Pamela had to let it out and this was the last time she would be this close to Veronica again; and she hated knowing that.

As the burial gathering came to a close many of the family and friends headed towards their cars. While Face talked to Quincy and his cousin King, he noticed a black limousine as it pulled up on the grounds. The burial was private and Face wasn't sure who this limo belonged to so all his men were put on notice to be cautious.

Three of Face's men rushed in front of him as the door to the limo opened and two men exited the vehicle. The men approached without delay and Face's crew began to draw their arms. Face instructed them to relax as the men dressed in black suits approached him with no concern for Face's men who had begun to point their weapons at them.

"Very sorry to interrupt you during your time of grieving sir, but Mr. Smith there is someone important that needs to speak with you," one of the man said. "Who would that be," Face asked. "Our boss Sir. I can't say who he is but you can trust that you'll be safe. That is our helicopter above and we have a count and lock on all your armed men. So if you'd just come with us we can guarantee you safety. If we wanted to hurt you we have more than enough man power to do it. We are here strictly for you to have a conversation with our boss."

"I'll be right back," Face said, upsetting everyone in his crew. They pleaded with Face to stay put and decline the invite but what they didn't realize was that Face had no choice. Not only was he curious to know who had been following him and had the man power to track and cover Face's crew, but he knew what the man had said was true. If they wanted him dead they could have killed him already.

Face followed the men to the limo and once he climbed inside he could not believe his eyes. "Wow," Face said, as he stared at The President of the United States of America. He had always been able to remain cool but to be sitting in the back of the presidential limo was grounds for him to be a bit speechless. "Yes, sometimes I have that effect on people," The President said. "Well how you are, it's good to meet you," Face said. "Nice to meet you as well," The President said as he shook his hand. "But I have a serious problem and that's why I'm here," The President continued. "What type of problem could you be having that would require my help," Face asked, assuming he was being sought out to assist the Commander in Chief.

"The C.O.U.P. is my problem. I know you've heard of them because I see you're connected to Vince, the private investigator, and we know his background. Some things that I do must always be political if I want to stay in the office and get reelected for another term. I know this organization is powerful but they are capable of taking a hit and being brought down a peg.

They threatened my family and they are ready to take out yours as well. You are a target as well and I'm here because I need you to take care of this for us. I want my freedom from them and you'll have your safety from them as well; if we work together."

Face was speechless. He was being asked to take on a task by The President of the United States. He was angered to hear the C.O.U.P. was still targeting him after he had dealt with Paul Warner but honestly he knew they wanted payback for their loss.

"So what can I do," Face asked. "They are on a retreat in Wisconsin for one of their annual gatherings. On this list are the names of the members and right now they are sitting ducks. I am asking you to help me with this problem…or let's say I'd like you to eliminate a common nemesis that we share. You will get your freedom and I will be in full control of my office," The President said as Face stared at the list.

"The Vice President, he's on the list," Face asked. He's the biggest problem. He's after you and my family. Can you handle this," The President asked. "I can handle it but I'm a business man…"Face said. "No favor goes unrecognized with me and I'll be in touch," The President said. "And I'm sure you understand the need of secrecy in this matter. Oh and you know how to get rid of evidence I'm sure. That paper does not exist," The President said.

"That goes without saying," Face said, as he shook The President's hand, took his list, and got out of the limo.

Everyone was waiting on Face's return, as the two men who had come with The President stood watch until Face got out of the limo. As he walked back to his crew, Reese asked, "Yo, who was that?" Face knew he needed to keep this under wraps and he said, "It was a good friend of Veronica's. He wanted to say his final goodbye to a family member and tell me how much he loved her."

As The President's limo left the cemetery the helicopter hovering above followed the car. Face had just been given information that could set him free from the problems that were threatening his family's way of life. He had a serious task at hand and if he didn't handle this he may be in a casket very soon.

Chapter 48
Two Days Later

Detective Murphy knew Norman "Face" Smith Jr. was in a league all his own. For two days he had been studying the man who was able to get acquitted when the evidence against his was stacked so high up against him that he could have gotten two life sentences. Detectives Murphy was not simply looking into Face but he was studying his crew as well. He had been looking into Gloria, Quincy, Reese, Kyle and a new name had been added to the pot, and that was of his first cousin Darius, "King" Smith; the former college basketball star who was rumored to be working for Face.

Detective Murphy knew that he couldn't get to Face directly but there was a chance for him to get to Face if he could break the chain. His back was against the wall as he tried to find a way to convict Face. There was no one in his crew willing to snitch and he knew those sex tapes were a Get-Out-Of-Jail-Free card if Face had access to them. However, the detective could not give up. He wanted Face to pay for murdering Ron Perry. This case was a sore spot and a blemish on the detective unit because it had not been solved. He was searching for a way to bring Face down and he wasn't going to stop until he had found one.

New York City

Inside of Gloria Jones' Law Offices, Face and Pamela watched as she unlocked the wall safe. Once the safe was opened Gloria pulled out six DVD's.

"All the tapes were converted over to digital formatting like you asked, Gloria said. "Thanks so much,"

Pamela said. For over five years the tapes had been kept there and only Pamela, Veronica and Gloria knew their hiding space. Face had been in the dark about where the tapes were and he was glad to finally have them.

Before leaving New York, Face and Pamela dined out with Gloria and Samaj. They enjoyed spending time with one another and after their driver dropped Gloria and Samaj off, they were headed back to Philadelphia.

Their limousine driver lifted up the separation glass and gave Pamela and his mother some privacy. "Are you okay," Pam asked her son. "I feel okay. It was good to spend some time with Samaj again," Face replied. "I want you to spend more time with that boy. He's your oldest and we have to keep our family tight. He looks just like you," Pam said, as a smile came to her face. "I will mom. I talked with Tasha and she knows I have some catching up to do," Face said. "Good. That's your son and I know you'll take care of everything as you should," she said, as she kissed her son on the cheek.

Face smiled as he reached into his pocket and pulled out his untraceable cellphone. He dialed a number and waited as it rung.

"Hello my brother," a voice said with a Latin accent. "Are your people in the country yet," Face asked. "Yes, we have been in the states for about twelve hours," the man said. "Good. I don't need any mistakes," Face instructed. "Don't worry my brother, I have six of the best men on it. I won't fail you my friend," the man said. "Great. Just call when everything is done. I'm counting on you," Face said as he hung up.

Pamela looked at her son and said, "Who was that?" Pamela had heard the conversation and wanted some real answers. She was worried about her family after losing Veronica and had to ask. "That's just a friend of mine," Face said. "From out of the county," she said. "Yes mom. I been stop being local. They're friends of mine that came here to help me out with a few things. Everything is fine mom. Relax."

Pamela wasn't going to ask any more questions because she knew her son was hiding certain details. They both had a lot on their plates and that last thing she wanted to do was frustrate her son with her worrying. As they continued on the way home, Face grabbed the remote control and they began to watch the movie, The Temptations. His mother loved watching that movie and was a big David Ruffin fan. Face got comfortable in his seat, as he pulled his mom close to him. "I love you mom," he said, as they drove on. "You better," she replied.

Chapter 49
10:23 P.M.
Sister Bay, Wisconsin

For the last two days twelve C.O.U.P. members had been in a secluded location in Wisconsin. They were staying in an exclusive lodge house with full amenities that was tucked away in a hidden wooded area. The fourteen bedroom lodge sat on twenty-eight acres of land, and was owned by The Vice President, Charles Bush. Three armed men guarded the facility as the C.O.U.P. members slept peacefully inside.

As the men patrolled the grounds they did not notice that they were being watched from behind the tall trees in the woods. Each of the men who had the guards in their scope had been armed with loaded weapons that would do nothing short of eliminate a target effortlessly. They had been given strict orders to kill every single member in the C.O.U.P. organization and if they failed their mission they were told to kill themselves, because they would be murdered on site.

The six men approached the lodge and were ready to take action. Three men took aim at the security detail as they hit all their targets with precision and proceeded to move forward.

Like a swarm of killer bees they entered the lodge and began to look for their honey. As they reached each member's bedroom, they entered but instead of using their guns they used a twelve inch knife and cut the throat of the C.O.U.P. members' throats as they slept. They were instructed to give out a signature Columbian necktie, so each member was sliced from ear to ear; as they bleed to death. Then just as a precaution that no one survived, the knife was then plunged into their chest and twisted to ensure the heart muscle had been punctured and disabled.

In less than ten minutes every one on the compound had been killed. Vice President Charles Bush, too, suffered the same fate as his comrades. A cell phone camera took a picture of his lifeless body and was sent to the men's boss. The mission had been completed and the team of Columbian hit men exited the home, disappearing into the darkness of the Wisconsin night.

Inside of the limo Face felt his phone vibrate. Pamela had fallen asleep and her light snores were enough to keep Face awake. "Hello," Face said, as he answered his phone. "The job is done. I'll send a nice photo to you," the man said as he hung up the phone.

Face waited anxiously for the message to come through. Within seconds he saw the slain body of Vice President Charles Busch and he breathed a sigh of relief. He deleted the message and his tired body was now able to relax enough for him to fall asleep next to his mother.

Medellin Columbia

Carlos Fuentes was the younger brother of former Columbian drug boss Roberto Fuentes. After the U.S. government murdered his brother he was next in line to take over the family business.

Two days earlier Carlos had received an emergency call from Face about an issue that he needed straightened out. Face never disclosed the secret conversations he had with The President but he provided Carlos with what he needed to successfully complete his task. Face gave Carlos the names and location of the

C.O.U.P. members after Carlos promised he was the man for the job. Not only did Carlos know the C.O.U.P. posed a threat to the family business but he had to have his revenge. Carlos wanted to ensure that everyone knew it was the Columbians who eliminated the C.O.U.P. so that's why it was important for them to all have the signature neckties.

As Carlos sat on the porch of his million dollar home, he puffed on a Cuban cigar and felt at ease. His brother's killers were no more and the world had been sent a message. Today had been a good day for him and as his dark black hair blew in the wind he smiled. He would be ever grateful to his new brother Face because he made it possible for Carlos to have his revenge. Yes, Face was his brother for life.

Chapter 50
Early The Next Morning
Washington, D.C

The news about the dead men and woman on the Wisconsin compound turned into a national and international media storm. Every network CNN, CNBC, ABC, BBC, CBS, MSNBC, had reporters staked out at the lodge; and viewers located in far as China were tuned in.

Washington D.C. had been placed on high alert and U.S. Marshalls was stationed all over the city. The President and his family were taken to a secured bunker beneath the White House. This was necessary because with the murder of The Vice President the impression was that the country was under attack. This was a required protocol that had to be taken to ensure the first family's safety. This was the biggest mass-murder conspiracy in the United States history and all protection was now placed around the Commanding Officer.

The world was stunned and in total disbelief. It was front page news on every newspaper in America. The F.B.I., C.I.A., and Homeland Security had their best agents descended Wisconsin. So far the only clue any of the agents had come from the way the men and woman were killed. The slice from ear to ear was a signature move of the Columbians but still they had no proof. Until they had something concrete they had to continue to investigate all possible leads.

The President and his family sat inside of the secure bunker with three members of their secret service staff. They were also accompanied by the Secretary of State, a five star general, and the U.S. Attorney General.

"Don't worry Sir, we will get to the bottom of this and find out who is behind this attack," Secretary of State John Wilson said. "We have every agency in our reach on top of this," he added. The President looked at the Secretary and said, "This is tragic beyond words. I want whosever responsible caught and convicted. Vice President Bush was a great man. A man filled with integrity and honor and I was lucky to have him as my VP. His legacy will live on in our hearts forever," The President said, as he took a short pause. "I won't rest until we find out who did this."

Everyone listened intently to the Commander in Chief. His words were spoken of a man who was hurting and suffering a grave lost. The emotions behind his words were intense and caused the members in the room to empathize and mourn with him. Unbeknownst to them The President was giving an Oscar winning performance. He had never been happier and the death of his VP gave him back the power he had rightfully earned.

Four Days Later
C.I.A. Headquarters
Langley, VA

A few miles west of Washington, D.C., was the home of the Central Intelligence Agency. Director of National Intelligence, John O. Brennan and four of his top supervisor were seated in the conference room.

"I just got word from The President. He wants us to put our focus on the Russians, The Columbians and the Taliban," John said. "I don't understand. Why don't we focus on everyone? This could have been an inside job. There were only a handful of people who knew where The VP was at. We've got people in our own backyard that might have been in on this. The drug lord in Philadelphia has been at the top of our F.B.I.'s and the N.S.I.'s list for years," one of the men said. "I'm relaying an official message from The President. We are to keep our focus on the parties named and you should follow rank. He's the Chief and you would do yourself good to remember who you're questioning," The director said, as he slightly scolded the supervisor. "Besides you're talking about a drug dealer with the ability to pull off a sophisticated hit like that. Are you serious," John said, as he brushed off the notion.

Pamela lay across her bed as she watched the CNBC news report of The Vice President's assassination. A strange feeling told her that Face had been connected to this case. She knew her son better than anyone and she knew he would not rest until he had gotten revenge on Veronica's murderer. The phone call Face had gotten while they were in the back of the limo from a friend assured her that her son had played his part in the death of Vice President Charles Bush.

A bright smile came on her face as she sipped from her glass of Moscato. She raised her glass in the air and said, "This one is for you Veronica. Face got them for you. I love you sister, sleep well."

Northeast Philadelphia

"Fuckem, that's what they get for slippin," Reese said to Quincy. They were sitting at a table counting the monetary contents of two duffle bags. A small television sat on the table as the news reporter from Fox talked about the tragic murders in Wisconsin. "We all slip at some point. It's hard to stay on go twenty-four seven," Quincy said, as he placed one hundred-thousand-dollars into one of the bags. "What, not me. I can smell when something ain't right. I'm always ready," Reese said. "Oh, you must get that from Face," Quincy said jokingly.

Reese became serious as he looked at Quincy and said, "No, Face get that shit from me and I'm tired of not gettin my credit!"

Three Weeks Later

The government was still searching for the people behind the killings of the C.O.U.P. members and the three guards. So far they had yet to finger a single suspect and they were been hammered in the press for not brining anyone to justice. Things did calm down a little in D.C. but the city was still on high alert. The President had been assigned extra security from the U.S. Marshals when he did press conferences; and even the regular reporters had to go through additional security to attend.

Now in full power, The President played his part to help his friend out in Philadelphia. All attention that had been formally placed on Face was stopped. It was a nice gesture and a well-deserved reward because Face had given The President the ability to play his true role as Commander in Chief. With Charles Bush gone the freedom to rule had been placed back into the hands of the man the people had elected.

The Philadelphia F.B.I. Office

After taking pictures of classified documents, Karen Brown excitingly walked from her place of employment and got into her car. Within ten minutes she had pulled up to the corner of 12th & Spring Garden

Streets. She parked and quickly got out of her car and into the waiting grey Dodge Magnum.

"Hey baby," she said, as she leaned over and gave Quincy a kiss. She brought up the pictures in her cell phone that she had just taken and showed them to Quincy. "These are the documents on Face. They came in this morning," she said. Quincy read the documents as he looked at the photos and a huge smile appeared on his face. "Why didn't you tell me," he asked, giving her a kiss on her lips. "Because, I wanted to let you read this," she said.

Quincy forwarded the pictures to Face's phone and his own, before he deleted them out of Karen's cellular. The classified document read as follows:

The United States Government and it's agencies under the F.B.I., C.I.A. D.E.A., HOMELAND security and the A.T.F. have official closed its seven year investigation into Norman "Face" Smith Jr. and his organization.

Our findings indicate that Mr. Smith is no longer a threat to our national security. Therefore case #121867 has been officially terminated and all previous records and files should be closed immediately.

Richard Lowery
F.B.I Executive Director

"It's over baby! They've closed the case on you guys so you don't have to worry anymore," Karen said jubilantly. Quincy sat in shock. He was grateful that he didn't have to look over his shoulder for snipers, Federal Agents or Marshalls. He was starting to feel lighter as he sat there. This was excellent news.

Chapter 51

"No problems brother. If that's who you want me to deal with from now on then I'll respect your wishes. But I do hope you reconsider your plans of retirement Face. The game needs men like you. You're strong and loyal and you know that's a dying breed," Carlos said into his cellphone. "Trust me, he'll do fine. I taught him everything he knows and what I didn't teach him he studied and learned on his own," Face replied. "Well good. The numbers stay the same and I'll treat him just as good as I've treated you," Carlos said. "Thank you. I really appreciate it. I will call you soon with more info. And remember stay low and out of the public's eye until this situation calms down a little more," Face warned. "I will. Take care brother," Carlos said, as they ended the call.

Face drove into his three car garage and parked his BMW next to the Mercedes. He was satisfied with his final decision and nothing and no one would change his mind. He was done with the game and now he was ready to pass the torch. Face's focus has to be on his family and healing their wounds. His son and daughter would need counseling and his newly united son may need some as well; to deal with the fourteen years absence of his father. There were pains that Tasha had suffered, as well as his mother, and they needed time to heal. Face wanted his family whole and the only way to be involved in their lives was to leave his other life behind. He was out.

Detective Roscoe Murphy had driven past Doc's house six times in the last two days. Doc's name had been passed off to him from an informant in West Philly. The snitch had told the detective that Doc was a key player in Face's organization, and that the two of them had been friends for many years.

Detective Murphy was desperate for information so whatever lead he got, he was going to follow. So far the only thing he had really learned about the doctor was that he was peculiar, white, and he lived in a neighborhood where Reese and Face had grown up in. He also found out Doc had been expelled from school but the reason listed was unknown. The institution also refused to elaborate on Doc's termination.

The detective was trying to put pieces of the puzzle together but he fell short continuously. He watched Doc's home and in two days he had only seen him come out and go to the store. He observed him, both times, as he walked with a blond haired woman. There was nothing strange about what he saw. There was nothing for him to suspect because everything about this man seemed legal.

As he got into his car and drove off the frustration he felt was pushing him to his breaking point. He had asked everyone he knew for help. He hit the streets and reviewed the paperwork on Face and his organization and still he had nothing that would warrant an arrest. He was back to square on.

A Few Days Later
Olive Garden Restaurant
City Avenue, Philadelphia

Inside of the crowded Italian restaurant, Face and Reese sat at a private table in the back of the establishment talking. Every so often the two would meet there to discuss business and to get something to eat. When Face received the text from Quincy, he was excited to sit down with Reese and have him look it over.

"It's all over Reese. The government has closed their case against us and we are now cleared," Face said, as he passed the phone over to Reese so he could review the document. "We can get out of this game together and move on with our lives. No more worries about getting shot at or locked away for life. Our families need us and this is the best time for us to take advantage of this," Face said, as he waited on Reese's response.

"Face I'm glad the case is closed but I'm not out. This is my life and I told you that a while ago. I'm not backing out of something I love. If you move on, then you move on but I'm in this forever. I'll never quit, it's just not what I do," Reese said. "Are you serious? You have everything you need and want, and you're still willing to risk it all? That's foolishness Reese and I know you're smarter than that. You need to think about your family. You're not in the game by yourself. This is a dead man's game but we got out alive. That should be a wakeup call," Face said. "No, I don't need a wakeup call. I'm in my reality and I understand if you can't handle that. We two different type of dudes. I'm not putting on no business suits and making mergers. I have to do what's in me. I love you man…but I'm all in," Reese said.

Face put a hundred dollars down on the table and he and Reese walked out. They both had lost their appetites and knew the chemistry between them had changed. Face couldn't respect Reese's decisions and Reese wasn't about to change his mind to please Face. He was his own man and had to do his own thing.

As they reached their parked cars, Reese said, "So I guess this is the end of our business." Face smiled at his friend and said, "Yeah. I'm out." The men were saying their final goodbyes as Face noticed a familiar face approaching them. Reese had his back turned to the man and before he could turn around two slugs from the loaded .357 flew into Reese's back. As Reese began to fall to the ground the man quickly approached him and momentarily stared at his body. Death was in his eyes. Face stood frozen. He had been completely caught off guard, as the man now directed his attention towards him. He aimed his gun at Face's head as the man's tears begin falling from his eyes. Then he put his gun in his pocket and ran through the lot full of parked cars.

Reese was dead and there was nothing Face could do. He stood there staring at his best friend and could not move. Reese had been hot tempered, he had been hard-headed but he had always been there for Face. As bystanders began to crowd around the body and screams for help echoed into the air, Face couldn't find it in him to do anything. Shock had taken over his entire body as his mind shut him down completely.

The cops arrived on the scene quickly and began to push the crowd back. The ambulance arrived but Reese was dead on arrival and they didn't try to resuscitate him. The cops asked Face if he had seen anything and if he knew who had shot Reese, but he lied. The truth was he didn't need the police to know who had taken his best friend and brother away from him. The man who had once been a trusted friend and employee had come back with a vengeance. Kyle had been plotting and waiting for weeks and today he had killed the man who had murdered his fiancé and unborn child.

One Week Later

Face was tired of funerals. He had said he was done with people he loved being taken from him so he wanted out of the game…but still Reese got caught up in it. It had taken Face a few days to realize that Reese was dead and even at the funeral he couldn't cry. He was in a daze. He knew he wasn't numb but he felt as if he was in denial.

The last time Face had saw Reese he wanted to slap some sense into him, but he wanted his friend alive. There was no amount of anger or disappointment for Reese's decisions to stay in the game that would have caused Face to wish death on his brother. All Face wanted was for Reese and he to get out alive, and to live as normal as possible…but Kyle had not only changed the game; he ended it for Reese.

Face got into the game to get wealthy, for the power and respect; and he had accomplished all of that. Yet there was no amount of wealth that could compensate him for the violence and losses he suffered. Momma, TJ, Veronica and now Reese had been casualties of the brutal drug game; and their deaths would leave a lasting ache in his soul. Face was one of the biggest Kingpins in U.S. history and now he had to put the game behind him. The torch would be passed and his family would be his only agenda.

Chapter 52
Three Days Later

Inside of Face's newly purchased home, he and Quincy sat inside of his home talking. "You still don't want me to get a crew and go after Reese's killer," Quincy asked. "No, we good," Face said. Quincy was confused but he had never questioned Face before, so he wouldn't start now. "Okay, then what are you going to do with the last shipment? It's pretty big," Quincy asked. "I told you I was done with it but I've come up with something," Face said. "Face, I've been thinking too. I don't want to do this with anyone else. If you're out, I'm out…but what have you come up with for this work," Quincy asked.

Before Face could answer Quincy the front doorbell rang. Face quickly walked over to the door and opened it. "Here is the plan," Face said to Quincy, as King walked into the living room to join them. Quincy smiled and looked at Face. "Good choice, I hope you're ready for this," Quincy said. "I been ready," King replied.

Face looked at King and said to him in all seriousness. "This game ain't no joke. You can't expect to win the war without some serious casualties. If loyalty is not in your blood than you don't belong here. Never lose who you are, don't ever lose your honor or what you stand for. It will save you, and know it's better that a man die with honor than to live as a coward. Stay loyal King and know I'm always here for you…but it's your throne now," Face said, as he hugged his young cousin. One legacy had just ended and another now began.

Six Months Later
George Town, Cayman

The Grand Cayman is the largest of the three Cayman Islands and it's located in the Western Caribbean Sea. Its beauty caught the attention of a man searching to relocate, and once Face had talked the move over with his wife, his entire family relocated to the tropical, exotic island. It was the perfect location for Face to start the next chapter of his life; and if he needed to get a taste of his homeland he could jump on his private jet and touchdown in Miami in about an hour-but for now he was happy with his choice.

Standing on the porch of his multi-million dollar beach villa, Face stared out at the bright shining sun and the beautiful blue ocean. He watched as his mother, wife, and children played a game of dodge ball. It was the first time in years the family felt free and at peace.

"A wonderful sight, huh," Quincy said, as he walked out of the house and onto the porch. "Yes, I've been waiting years for this and I didn't even know it," Face said, as Quincy sat down with him. "How are things working out with King," Quincy asked. "He's doing good. I check on him from time to time, and so far it's been all positive," Face said, as he smiled.

Quincy looked over at Face and looked him in the eyes and said, "So it's really over?" After taking a deep breath Face replied, "Sometimes I wonder if it is myself. I had a few dreams and each time I was back in the game, but then I sit out here and see my family and say no way." Quincy smiled and said, "Yeah, I've been having dreams too.. I guess the game is in our blood. If you're ever needed would you go back," Quincy asked. Face thought about it and said, "Only God knows the answer to that."

Coming Soon

DASAINT ENTERTAINMENT

PRESENTS

KING

A

NOVEL

JIMMY DASAINT

"ANOTHER CLASSIC NOVEL FROM THE NEW KING OF URBAN FICTION"
– HORIZON BOOKS

DASAINT ENTERTAINMENT ORDER FORM

Please visit www.dasaintentertainment.com to place online orders.

You can also fill out this form and sent it to:
DASAINT ENTERTAINMENT
PO BOX 97
BALA CYNWYD, PA 19004

TITLE	PRICE	QTY
BLACK SCARFACE	$15.00	_____
BLACK SCARFACE II	$15.00	_____
BLACK SCARFACE III	$15.00	_____
BLACK SCARFACE IV	$15.00	_____
YOUNG RICH & DANGEROUS	$15.00	_____
WHAT EVERY WOMAN WANTS	$15.00	_____
THE UNDERWORLD	$15.00	_____
A ROSE AMONG THORNS	$15.00	_____
A ROSE AMONG THORNS II	$15.00	_____
CONTRACT KILLER	$15.00	_____
MONEY DESIRES & REGRETS	$15.00	_____
ON EVERYTHING I LOVE	$15.00	_____
SEX SLAVE	$15.00	_____
THE DARKEST CORNER	$15.00	_____
AINT NO SUNSHINE	$15.00	_____
WHO	$15.00	_____

Make Checks or Money Orders out to:
DASAINT ENTERTAINMENT

NAME: ______________________________________

ADDRESS: ___________________________________

____

CITY: ____________________________ STATE: ____
ZIP:_______________ PHONE:_________________

INMATE ID #:________________________________
$3.50 for each book to cover shipping and handling cost
($4.95 For Expedited Shipping per item)
WE SHIP TO PRISONS!!!

29989455R00114

Made in the USA
Middletown, DE
09 March 2016